MURDER WESTERN STYLE

A Sister Sleuths Mystery: Book 3

Rayna Morgan

Chapter One

When Lea and Maddy arrived at the fairgrounds, the parking lot was already filling with cars. In the small coastal town where they lived, the annual rodeo was a popular event.

"Thanks for inviting me, Sis," Lea said, watching the swarms of people streaming in. "Believe it or not, this is my first rodeo."

"Shame on you, girl. You've been missing out until you've seen steer wrestling and bronc riding."

"I tried to get Paul to come, but he's playing in the softball tournament today," Lea said.

"You made the right choice. Rodeos are more exciting than softball games. Watching all these cowboys walking around in their chaps isn't hard on the eyes either." Maddy laughed, shaking her long brunette hair as she pulled on a cowboy hat.

She nodded toward a man in front of them carrying a saddle. He turned in time to catch her stare. "Don't flatter yourself, cowboy," she said, peering over the rim of her sunglasses. "I was looking at your boots."

His smile broadened as he tipped his hat and moved away.

Flustered, Maddy looked toward the rodeo arena. "There's Katie."

She waved at a girl dressed in a red-and-black plaid shirt, a black hat with a silver band, and leather boots with fancy red-and-black stitching.

"Look at you!" Maddy said, wrapping her arms around the twelve-year-old. "You've got to be the prettiest cowgirl at the rodeo. You must be breaking plenty of young cowboys' hearts today."

The girl's cheeks turned rosy as Maddy turned to her sister.

"Katie Miller, this is my sister. Lea, this is Scott's daughter."

"Nice to meet you, ma'am," the girl said, extending her hand before poking Maddy. "It's not my looks that will bring home the Junior Cowgirls trophy. It's all my hard training. I hope it pays off."

She looked older than her age except for the string of freckles splashed across her nose. "We only have three more events to qualify for the finals. I have a chance to rack up a bunch of points today."

"Don't worry, sweetie," Maddy said, "you'll knock 'em dead."

Anxious to find her horse and get mounted, Katie pulled Maddy's hand. "I can't wait to get started. Dad's waiting for us at the horse trailer."

* * *

Lea and Maddy glimpsed the grandstand where people were filing in to find seats, anxious to cheer on their favorite contestants. Passing the concession area, they inhaled the aroma of hamburgers sizzling on the grill, brisket simmering in a smoker, and marinated ribs grilling. The sounds of men calling out and horses whinnying surrounded them. They inhaled the peppery, spicy smells coming from the tent where the barbecue cook-off was being held.

"Think your dad can get us into that tent later?" Maddy asked, drooling.

"All the contestants get tickets to the barbecue," Katie said.

"One of my customers is a judge for the cook-off," Maddy said. "I told her if she could get me on that judging panel next year, I'd give her a discount on the next piece of furniture she buys."

"Is your dad entered in any competitions today?" Lea asked Katie, ignoring her sister's food rantings.

"He's in the shooting contest. Dad's the best shooter in the county," the girl beamed. "He's won the event the last five years in a row and—"

Katie was interrupted by the sound of loud voices as they neared an area filled with campers and trailers. Maddy pulled the girl up short as she and Katie recognized a voice belonging to her father.

"Back off, Albert. You're being a jerk. This is a friendly competition. Let's keep it fun for our kids."

"Don't think for a minute your daughter's beating my girl today," the other voice snarled. "Lucy can ride rings around Katie any day of the week. Your kid only wins events because she gets preferential treatment due to your position on the board of the Cattlemen's Association."

"That's our neighbor, Albert Benson," Katie whispered. "I'm riding against his daughter today. Lucy and I are friends, but her father always tries to pit us against each other. He turns everything Lucy does into a competition. He embarrasses her in front of the kids at school."

Lea and Maddy crouched and moved closer so they could see the man Katie was referring to.

"That's not true, Albert," Scott said. "Katie gets everything she earns through hard work."

Maddy noted the crimson color flooding Katie's face, but Lea's attention stayed riveted on the man Katie called their neighbor.

His thin body shook, contorted in angry spasms. His jaws tightened as he spewed venom. "Your family's been throwing their weight around this county for years. But my daughter's going to take all of you down a peg when she whips your daughter in the Junior Championship. There will be one less trophy for you to display on your mantel."

With an ugly sneer, the man spat a wad of chewing tobacco on the ground in front of Scott, spattering the cowboy's boots. His arm swung out in a misdirected punch.

"Dad, no," Katie screamed, a moment too late. Her father landed a hammer blow hard enough that Albert fell to the ground.

Scott wheeled around, surprised to see his daughter running toward him. "What are you doing here?" He stooped on one knee to put an arm around her. She was clearly shaken by the violent exchange.

"Albert and I were just airing a difference of opinion. It got out of hand. It's all right; no damage done."

"No damage done, you SOB?" Albert yelled, brushing away the hand Scott extended to help him to his feet. "You may have cracked my tooth."

"You brought it on yourself," Scott said.

"Says who?" Albert asked, sarcastically.

"Beg your pardon, sir," Maddy said, advancing toward the man as he brushed soil from his pants. "We saw the whole thing. You looked to me like a man poking a stick at a bear. You should have known to stop before you made the grizzly mad."

The man glared at Maddy. "Butt out, lady."

"Don't disrespect the woman," Scott warned.

"Get out of my way," Albert yelled, pushing past Scott. "But don't think for a moment this is over."

Katie clung to her father as their neighbor stomped away. "Are you okay, Dad?"

Scott looked at the red welt spreading across his knuckles and shuffled his feet. "I'm sorry you all saw that. It was uncalled for on my part. I shouldn't have let the fool get to me that way. My apologies to you and your sister, Maddy."

"I'm beginning to see why Maddy says rodeos are exciting," Lea said.

"And you haven't even seen the bull riding," Maddy said.

They all laughed before Scott turned and headed toward a trailer calling over his shoulder. "C'mon, Katie. Let's get you ready for the barrel racing. Chief's all saddled up and raring to go."

"Is your ride today the Chumash Indian chief who lives on your ranch?" Maddy asked, teasing dimples out of the girl as they followed Scott to the horse trailer.

"No, silly." Katie giggled. "Chief gave me a colt when we moved back to the ranch from Colorado. I named the horse in his honor. That horse and I have been together every day since."

Maddy turned to Scott as he held a stirrup and boosted Katie into the saddle. "We hear you'll be competing today."

"I might try my hand at the mounted shooting," he said, pushing his hat back on his head.

"Katie told us you're the champion," Lea said.

Scott looked at his daughter. Pride shone in her face.

"Now, girl. What have I told you about sounding boastful?" her father said, but his eyes sparkled as he pulled at her braided ponytail. "Go get 'em, girl. We'll be rooting you on from the stands. Have fun."

The three adults watched the girl and the horse gallop away in a synchronized, fluid motion.

* * *

"That was quite a dust-up you had with the other rancher," Maddy said, as they headed toward the arena.

"Oh, that's just Albert being Albert. He always walks around with a chip on his shoulder. I shouldn't have let him get under my skin."

"He sounds real competitive where his daughter's concerned."

"He's always pushing his kids to win. He uses them to compensate for how unfairly he thinks life has treated him."

"Unfairly how?" Lea asked.

"Life dealt him a hand that turned him bitter. His wife, Victoria, died in childbirth. She had a hard time with the birth of their son, Dalton. The doctor told her she shouldn't have more children, but Albert wanted another son. The second time, she wasn't so lucky. Albert felt double cursed when the baby his wife died delivering wasn't the second son he wanted. He got a daughter: Katie's friend, Lucy."

"The way I see things, pain is pretty much a guaranteed part of life," Maddy said. "Suffering is up to the individual."

"I can't fault your take on things, Maddy," Scott said and smiled, "but I don't think anything will be changing Albert anytime soon. Let's not let it spoil our day. We've got time to grab lunch before Katie's first event. Let me treat you two to some mouth-watering barbecue."

* * *

An hour later, their appetites satisfied, Scott, Maddy, and Lea took seats in the arena near the front where they would be easily visible to Katie as she rode past. They turned their attention to the voice coming over the loudspeaker announcing the riders for the barrel racing.

Maddy sneezed, inhaling the dust rising from the arena as the horses galloped around the ring.

Scott grinned. "Sounds like someone's going to have a stuffy nose tonight."

"It's all good," Maddy replied. "I'll take rodeo dust over smog any day of the week."

When Katie's name was announced, she rode into the middle of the arena, waving her hat over her head and smiling in their direction.

Lucy Benson's name was called next. Several moments passed without Albert's daughter making an entrance. Her name was repeated over the loudspeaker, and she still didn't appear. The announcer issued a warning the contestant would be scratched from the competition if she didn't appear momentarily.

Scott mumbled under his breath. "Has that fool wasted so much time bragging up his daughter that they've missed the competition? I'll go round them up."

At last, the starting gun went off signaling the start of the contest. There was still no sign of Lucy, and Scott hadn't returned.

"Katie would want you to see her," Lea said, patting her sister's knee. "I'll go look for them."

Lea left to search for Scott, and Maddy watched alone as Katie raced around the barrels.

* * *

Running into the campground, Lea saw Scott standing beside a young girl she knew must be Lucy Benson. They stood motionless, staring at the ground in front of them.

"What's the holdup?" Lea asked, coming up behind them. "What's happened?"

"Dad, oh my gawd, Dad," the girl sobbed.

Lea saw the answer to her question: Albert Benson's body lying face up in the dust, blood seeping slowly across the front of his shirt.

Scott's arm encircled the shaking girl. He looked at Lea; shock registered on his face. "I'll get her away from here."

Lea punched in the emergency number on her cell phone as she followed Scott to his camper.

Lucy slumped into a chair beside a small dining table. The color had drained from her face, and her body shivered.

Scott pulled a blanket from a cupboard and tried to wrap it around the girl, but she pulled away sharply. "Leave me alone. My father hated you. He was always telling Dalton and me about how you and your family try to control things. Now he's dead. I never want to see you or your family again."

The girl flung open the door of the camper and ran out, crashing into Katie and Maddy coming up the stairs. She hurled herself against a tree, sobs racking her slender body.

Scott started after the girl, but Katie grabbed his arm. "Don't, Dad. She's upset. I'll take her to find Dalton."

Scott leaned against the door-frame, shaking his head.

"What was that all about?" Lea asked, referring to the angry words the girl had spoken.

"Old history. Nothing that has anything to do with what happened here today. Lucy's out of her head right now."

Before Lea could question Scott further, police sirens pierced the air shattering the eerie silence that had settled in around the prone body.

"I'll go," Maddy said. "You two wait here."

* * *

Scott offered Lea a cup of coffee before pulling a bottle of whiskey from a shelf in the cupboard.

"That was rough," he said. "Want a swig in your brew?"

"No, thanks. I'll wait until I get home. I should call my husband to let him know what's happened."

"Probably a good idea," Scott said. "Maddy's mentioned Paul on several occasions. I'd like to meet him, but not under these conditions."

"As far as my husband's concerned, my sister and I have been around conditions like these too frequently. He won't be a happy camper when he hears about this."

"Does your sister always attract trouble?" Scott asked, smiling. "This is the third time she and I have been entangled in a dicey situation."

"She has been called somewhat of a drama queen. Speaking of drama, what was Lucy saying about your family and her father being at odds?"

"Benson and my family have never seen eye to eye on the wild mustangs. Our view is mustangs aren't meant to be tamed; they should be left to roam free. My neighbor didn't want his cows sharing the grazing land with wild horses. He wanted the BLM to control them."

"The BLM?"

"Bureau of Land Management. It's a federal agency tasked with protecting wild horses and cattle and their grazing lands. The agency's idea of managing the land in this state has been to round up the mustangs and sell them, supposedly ensuring the horses go to good homes and aren't slaughtered."

"Are you suggesting some of the horses sold by the BLM end up being sent to slaughterhouses?"

"I'm more than suggesting it. My family brought charges against one rancher we knew was doing it. The agency finally launched an investigation, but it was only due to the public outrage created at the hearing. The BLM never admitted culpability, but they stopped doing business with the rancher."

"How awful." Lea cringed. "Does Lucy understand the issue between the two of you? It's hard to believe she would side with her father."

"I doubt Albert discussed it with her. He doesn't share his point of view unless he's sure the person agrees with him. Lucy would never have agreed with him about the mustangs. She loves them as much as Katie does."

* * *

When Tom Elliot got out of an unmarked vehicle, Maddy wasn't surprised. Tom was head of the Homicide and Major Crimes Division of the Buena Viaje Police Department, so murder was his bailiwick. With his six feet three inches of toned physique, sun-bleached blond hair, and gray eyes with the satin finish of brushed steel, he was also one of the most eligible bachelors in town.

What did surprise her was that he was already back on the job after a well-deserved vacation, three days of which she and Tom had spent relaxing in the wine country.

"Embroiled in crime so soon?" she asked, taking deep breaths to calm her shattered nerves as she walked to greet him. "I thought you had two more vacation days you were using to work on your car."

"Murder doesn't take a holiday just because I do. Besides, working on my car is exactly what the term implies: work. Solving crime is my passion."

"Is solving crime the only thing you're passionate about?" she asked, the corners of her mouth turning up into a coquettish smile.

"Don't distract me." He frowned. "What are you doing here? I suppose the cowboy invited you."

"If you're referring to Scott," she replied, noting Tom's sarcastic tone of voice, "it was his daughter, Katie, who invited Lea and me. She wanted us to watch her compete in the Junior Cowgirls Championship."

Tom looked around. "Who found the body?"

"The victim's daughter, Lucy. Katie has taken her to find her brother."

"They shouldn't have left the crime scene. I need to talk to them, pronto."

"I'll tell Scott to call Katie on her cell phone."

"Where is he?"

"He and Lea are in the camper. Lea's upset." She took a step before her knees buckled.

Tom grabbed her, pulling her against his chest. "Whoa, you're a little shaky yourself. Are you okay?"

"Nothing a shot of tequila and a good night's sleep won't cure."

A grin spread slowly over Tom's face like syrup over waffles. "You need some company?"

"For the shot of tequila," she asked, "or the good night's sleep?"

"Either one," he said, pushing a strand of hair from her eyes, "or both."

"Lieutenant, over here," a man's voice hollered.

"Go do your job." Maddy snickered, breaking eye contact and turning away.

"Tell Lea and the cowboy I'll be over to take their statement," Tom said.

Maddy watched him kneel to examine the body and heard him barking orders as she walked away.

"Okay, let's get this thing rolling. Sergeant Jones, cordon off the scene and look for the murder weapon. Fisher, get statements from everyone who knew the victim including anyone on the fairgrounds he came into contact with. I'll start with the folks in the camper as soon as the girls return."

* * *

Moments later, two young girls appeared, their arms wrapped around each other. They skirted the covered body, making a beeline for the camper.

Tom bumped into Maddy as he entered the trailer. The space was barely large enough for six people.

"Where's the brother? Did the girls find him?" he asked her.

"His car's here, but he's not. They came back without him when Scott called them."

Tom looked at the girls, huddled together, hands clasped. Katie's father stood beside them offering comfort and support.

The detective knew Scott Miller from his presence at two previous altercations in which Maddy was involved. He also knew Maddy's friendship with the cowboy had grown since their initial encounter when Miller rescued her from the clutches of a ruthless kidnapper.

He nodded in Scott's direction. "Is showing up at crime scenes getting to be a habit with you?"

"Our paths do seem to keep crossing," Scott replied, moving across the room to shake hands.

Tom ignored the response, uncertain as to whether it referred to the crime scenes or the friendship with Maddy they had in common.

"I need to speak with the girls. I'm told the daughter found the body."

"That's right. Let me introduce you." Scott put an arm around each of the girls, turning them to face the detective. "Lieutenant Elliot, this is my daughter, Katie. And this is Lucy Benson, Albert's daughter."

"I understand this has been a terrible shock for both of you," Tom said, straddling a chair and leaning over the back of it to be at eye level.

He spoke in a low tone, his voice kind. "I need your help to find out how this happened. Lucy, we'll start with you. Why were you and your father at the campground? Weren't you competing in the barrel competition?"

"I had my horse saddled and was waiting for my father to walk me into the arena. When the announcer started calling names and Dad hadn't shown up, I tied my horse up and went to find him. I had almost reached our trailer when I saw him on the ground and ran toward him. When I saw the blood..." Her voice hiccupped with a sob.

"Did you see anyone around your trailer? Maybe you heard something."

"I don't remember anything until Mr. Miller was standing next to me, staring down at my dad." Tears streamed down her face.

Tom turned to Scott. "I didn't realize you were at the scene."

"When Lucy didn't appear for her event, I went looking for her. I found her as she described: frozen in place, staring at the body. I could see her father was dead. When Lea came, she called the police while I got Lucy out of there. Maddy and my daughter came as soon as the contest ended."

Tom turned to Katie. "Did you see Mr. Benson before the competition?"

"Only when he was arguing with my father and Dad punched him." Pride sounded in her voice until she realized what she had said. She turned to Scott, an alarmed look in her eyes.

"Don't worry, kiddo. I'll tell the detective about my fight with Albert."

Tom grabbed Scott's elbow and steered him away from the girls. "Let's hear it. You can start by telling me about the victim."

"The Bensons are neighbors of ours."

"What happened here doesn't seem very neighborly." Tom's tone had a sharp edge.

"Albert's a local rancher." Scott's voice faltered. "Guess I should say, he was a local rancher. He kept a small herd of livestock and a couple hundred acres of crops. He tried raising ostriches a couple of years back, but it didn't pan out for him."

"Did he have any bad habits like drugs or gambling? Money problems?"

"I'm sure he didn't have a fortune stashed away, but he was holding his own, like most of the farmers in this economy."

"Was he mad at anyone?" Tom asked. He added, with sarcasm dripping, "I mean, anyone besides you?"

"I don't know of enemies, if that's what you're asking, but he wasn't well liked. He was a hothead, always blowing off steam." Scott looked in Lucy's direction. "He was tough on his kids, too, always a hard thing for people to watch."

"You mean child abuse?"

"I wouldn't go that far, but he worked them hard with chores and pushed them to win every competition they entered. Never let them be kids."

"Is that what your fight today was about?"

"Albert was spouting hot air about his kid being better than mine. When he insinuated Katie wins competitions because of my position on the Cattlemen's Association, I'd had enough. He threw a punch, and I decked him."

"Sounds like you're a bit of a hothead yourself."

"I'm not the only one. Plenty of people knew sometimes the only way to get Albert to shut up was to shut him up."

"All right, that's enough for now. Can you take Lucy home to her mother?"

"Lucy doesn't have a mother at home. Victoria Benson died. Albert was raising Lucy and her brother, Dalton, as a single parent."

"That's rough. How old is her brother?"

"Nineteen."

"So he can apply to be her legal guardian. That should make things easier than child services taking over. Do they have any other family around here?"

"Not that I know of, but I'll ask them about relatives. I'm sure Dalton will want to take care of his sister himself. From what I know of the boy, he's capable enough."

"All three of you need to come to the station tomorrow to sign statements unless you prefer Officer Fisher comes to your ranch."

"I'd appreciate that. It will be much less intimidating for the girls."

There was an edge to Tom's voice when he asked his next question. "Will you be taking Maddy home, too?"

"I would, but she came on her own." Scott's lips turned up in a sly grin. "You don't have anything to worry about. She was my daughter's guest, not mine."

* * *

"Looks like we've found the murder weapon, Lieutenant," Sergeant Jones hollered.

"What have you got?" Tom asked, approaching the officer.

"A rancher's horse was acting up. When the man found what was causing the ruckus, he called me over." He pointed to a pistol lying in the bushes next to the horse trailer. The two officers squatted over the gun. Jones put on disposable gloves, picked up the weapon, and dropped it into an evidence bag.

"Was the rancher able to identify it?"

"Said it was probably one of the pistols riders use in the shooting competition. That would be the only reason for anyone here to have a gun."

"What are these notches on the grip? They look like kill notches."

"I asked about those. Some competitors carve a notch in the handle of a gun when they win a shooting championship."

"If that's the case, it will help identify the owner of the gun. We're looking for someone who's won five times."

"That won't be hard to do."

Tom turned toward the voice of the man standing behind him. Jones made the introduction. "This is the owner of the trailer who found the gun."

"Thanks for bringing it to our attention," Tom said, shaking hands with the man. "It always helps when we locate the murder weapon at the outset of the investigation."

"As I said, those shooting matches are very competitive. Hard to score many wins before a new up-and-comer challenges your title."

"Anyone around here fit the bill?"

"Only one I know of."

"Who would that be?"

"Scott Miller. Best shooter in these parts by a mile."

* * *

Tom found Scott helping Katie load her horse. "One more thing before you head out."

"What can I do for you?" Scott asked, raising the tailgate on the trailer.

"Can I have a look at the pistols you used in the shooting competition?"

Scott looked up, surprised. "The competition isn't until this afternoon. With all that's happened, I hadn't thought about it. I need to withdraw from the contest before we leave."

"Where do you keep your guns?"

"In a storage unit in the back of the truck."

"Would you get them out, please?"

"Sure, no problem. I'll get the keys from the pegboard."

Moments later, Scott returned from the camper empty-handed. "Katie, where are the keys to the toolbox?" he asked.

"I don't have them, Dad."

The men looked at each other. Scott rushed to the back of the truck and pulled open the door. On the floor was an open metal box containing one pearl-handled pistol.

"Thought people used two guns in those competitions," Tom said.

"I do. The other gun should be here," Scott said, shuffling through oily rags.

"Are you saying someone stole your gun?"

"There's no other explanation. No one handles the pistols before a match but me. Katie's not allowed to handle guns."

"Could that gun have been used to kill Albert Benson?" Tom asked.

"Hardly. We don't use real bullets. The cartridges are filled with black powder. Live rounds are prohibited."

"But someone could have substituted a live round for the black powder in your gun, isn't that right?"

Scott hesitated before answering. "I suppose."

The detective looked at the other man with steely eyes. "It will be me coming to interview you at your ranch tomorrow instead of Officer Fisher."

* * *

Tom saw Lea and Maddy headed for the parking lot. He grabbed Maddy's arm as she unlocked her car. "You neglected to tell me about your cowboy's altercation with the victim."

Maddy turned abruptly, pulling his hand from her arm. "What are you talking about? You're hurting me."

"Exactly what I said. Why didn't you tell me Scott and the victim had a blowout shortly before Benson was found murdered?"

Maddy's face turned crimson. "What you're implying is absurd. If you think Scott Miller had anything to do with that man's death, you're plain loco."

"Calm down. I'm not accusing anyone of anything, yet. But you of all people should know information about a victim's actions or state of mind prior to his death is relevant."

"The minor scuffle that occurred earlier was the furthest thing from my mind when you arrived at the scene. If I thought you needed to know, don't you think I would have passed that information on to you?"

Tom hesitated, staring deeply into her eyes. "Honestly, Maddy, I don't know. I don't know how into this guy you are. Or for that matter, how into me you are. I don't know where your loyalties lie anymore."

"You better figure it out if you expect our friendship to stay intact," she said, slamming the car door. "I'm going home. This rodeo has been one rough ride."

Chapter Two

"Do you want to come in for a glass of wine?" Lea asked as Maddy drove into the driveway.

"A shot of tequila would be more like it," Maddy said, locking the car and following Lea into the house. "Maybe you're getting used to seeing dead bodies, but I'm not."

"Jon, you home?" Lea called out to her son.

"Looks like he left a note." Maddy pointed to a piece of paper on the dining room table. "Did he lose his cell phone again? Why didn't he just call you?"

"He leaves a note if he's not sure my answer will be yes." Lea smiled as she read the note. "This would have been a safe call."

She looked to the patio door where two dogs pressed their noses against the glass. "Let the dogs in. I'll fix our drinks."

Maddy opened the screen door, and the dogs bounded through. "Hey, Gracie," she said, acknowledging exuberant barks of affection from the yellow-and-white border collie.

"How you doing, Spirit?" she asked, handing the white golden retriever a treat from the canister on the counter. Following the dog out to the patio, she noted the smattering of soil on his paws. "Has Spirit been helping you with the gardening?"

Lea placed drinks on the patio table and sank into a wicker chair, brushing curls of copper hair off her brow. "If that's what you call digging holes. I see the rosebush is now leaning to the left. It didn't look that way when I left this morning. I need to channel his energy more productively."

Maddy raised a glass filled with orange-and-red liquid in the air. "Here's to murder, western style."

She smiled but her eye twitched, a telltale sign she was upset. A tremor ran through her body, and tears welled in her eyes.

"Are you okay?" Lea asked, reaching an arm across the table.

"I was keeping it together for the sake of the girls. Seeing a dead body is starting to sink in. That was too close to home."

"What was Tom saying to you at the car? He looked upset."

"He accused me of withholding knowledge of the argument between Scott and the victim."

Lea peered over her sunglasses. "Did you?"

"Not intentionally. I was caught up in the emotion of the moment. I wasn't thinking clearly."

"You weren't reluctant to give Tom information that might paint Scott in an unfavorable light?"

Maddy paused, twisting a strand of hair between her fingers. "I'm afraid that brush stroke has already been swiped. Considering Tom's feelings about Scott, it's not painting a pretty picture."

"You could be right."

Maddy sat back, tapping her fingernail on a tooth. "We've got to help Scott. You've had firsthand experience with what Tom's like once he gets a target in his sights; he can be downright mule-headed. If he thinks Scott's his man, he'll go after him as doggedly as Spirit chasing a rabbit."

"That's not true, and you know it. Tom goes where the facts lead him. You're worried his personal feelings will blind him to the facts in this case. You and I both know Tom well enough to know he won't let that happen. He'll only make a move based on the merits of the case."

Maddy chewed her lip. "Are you talking about motive, means, and opportunity?"

"That's exactly what I mean."

"There's the rub," Maddy said.

Lea arched her eyebrows. "You aren't saying—"

"Scott may have had all three; at least, from Tom's perspective he did. That's why we need to help."

"You're going to have to trust Tom to be fair." Lea crossed her arms in front of her. "I'm sorry for Scott, but I can't get involved. You know how Paul hates our sleuthing. He only got over our last venture because we solved the murder, so Tom forgave us for butting into his case."

"C'mon, Lea. If you won't do this for Scott, do it for us. This wasn't a three-minute spot we watched on the nightly news; we were there. A man's body was lying lifeless less than two feet in front of us. We saw Lucy's tears. We felt Katie's horror. Don't you want to learn the truth of what happened at the fairgrounds today?"

"I'm sorry, Mad." Lea's voice held a note of finality. She walked toward the kitchen.

Maddy stood up and planted her hands on her hips. "I find it ironic and more than a little maddening that when your friend Angelo was in Tom's cross-hairs, you had no qualms about getting me involved," she said, blowing a wisp of hair from her eyes, "without my knowledge or consent I might add. When my friend's in trouble, you throw up ridiculous excuses."

Lea turned swiftly, her eyes throwing daggers. "Are you trying to guilt me into getting involved in this case? Keeping peace with my husband is hardly a ridiculous excuse. Paul's made it clear how he feels about our adventures, or misadventures, as he calls them."

Maddy's pitch dropped a notch. "Sorry. Didn't mean to bad-mouth your concern over Paul's feelings, but this is important to me."

"I understand," Lea said. "But—"

"Besides," Maddy continued, in an effort to ward off further objections, "what kind of karma will I attract if I don't try to protect the man who saved my life? Would you expose me to a future plagued by demons?"

Lea's shoulders relaxed. A small smile played on her lips. "Your acting skills were short-lived in the theatre, but they're not wasted on me. What do you have in mind?"

* * *

Paul walked in the back door. Grabbing a bottled water from the refrigerator, he joined Lea and Maddy on the patio.

"How did you like the rodeo?" he asked, leaning to kiss the top of his wife's head. "I missed your call earlier, but you didn't leave a message. I thought you were spending the whole day there."

"Our plans were interrupted."

"Mine, too," Paul said, petting the dogs. "Tom and I were supposed to get a brew after our game. He left a message that he couldn't make the game, something about a new case."

"A case that ruined our day," Lea said.

"I thought Tom was still on vacation."

"I wish he would have stayed on vacation," Maddy said under her breath.

"Okay, what's going on?" Paul asked, looking toward Lea for an answer.

"Let Maddy explain." Lea shrugged. "It involves her friend."

Paul and Lea turned in unison toward Maddy who threw her hands in the air. "All right, Paul. I'll tell you what happened, but don't jump all over me. I swear it's just a matter of being in the wrong place at the wrong time."

"Did you ever consider it could be your willingness to put yourself, and my wife I might add, in precarious situations?"

"You mean I attract trouble?"

"Something like that," Paul said.

"Oh, c'mon, Paul," Lea said. "Give Maddy a chance to tell the story. Neither of us could have prevented what happened."

Paul sat down and folded his arms across his chest. "I'm all ears."

* * *

Maddy re-created the morning's events, finishing by saying, "So you see, Lea and I could hardly have avoided being involved."

"Except by the company you were keeping."

"Are you referring to Scott?" Maddy asked, anger creeping into her voice.

"You're upset because Tom has reason to cast a suspicious eye in his direction. But ask yourself how often Tom's been wrong. He didn't get to be where he is in the department by making mistakes in judgment."

Lea intervened to calm the tension in the air. "And Tom is your best friend, Paul. Don't take sides against each other in defense of your own friends."

"You're right. I may be overreacting because I'm waiting for the other shoe to fall." There was no response, so Paul continued. "Tell us the reason you're here, Maddy. Aren't you trying to talk Lea into helping you get your friend off the hook by finding the real killer?"

The sisters looked at each other. Neither dared take a breath.

"I told her I couldn't help," Lea said, running the back of her hand over Paul's clenched jaw.

"Has it occurred to either of you that you don't know who you're involved with?"

Maddy scowled at Paul. "You don't have to include Lea in your insinuation. You've always felt I used bad judgment marrying Eric. But I knew the man I was marrying. I knew he'd left his wife for me so there was a chance he'd leave me the same way. My marriage ended in divorce. It doesn't mean I'm a bad judge of character. It means I make my own decisions, and I'm willing to live with any consequences of the decisions I make."

"I think what Paul meant to say," Lea said, frowning at her husband, "is that you've only known Scott a few months. You don't know much about him."

"I know he's incapable of murder."

"Don't waste your breath, sweetheart," Paul told his wife, casting a despairing glance in Maddy's direction. He added under his breath, "And she calls Tom stubborn."

Maddy pinched her lower lip. "I met Scott when he saved me from a life-threatening situation. Are you suggesting the same person who saved my life could snuff out another person's life, especially the father of his daughter's close friend?"

"From what you related," Paul said, "there was bad blood between Scott's family and the victim. You can't ignore that. Neither will Tom."

"If Tom's trying to build a case, he may be inclined to take that information at face value," Lea said. "It couldn't hurt to determine how much truth there is to the allegation."

Resignation showed on Paul's face. "Since the object of those rumors is no longer available to shed light on the allegation, who do you propose as a source to determine the truth?"

"Someone known for his honesty and integrity," Maddy replied. "A man we can all trust."

* * *

Maddy called Katie's cell phone later that evening. When she answered, the girl's voice sounded tired but chipper.

"How are you doing, sweetie?" Maddy asked.

"I'm okay. Dad invited Dalton and Lucy to stay with us for a few days. They're sleeping in the guest house while Dad helps them sort out the funeral. We all had a sit-down dinner with Gram and Great-Granddad tonight."

Maddy made a mental note to inform her sister of Scott's gestures, hardly those of a murderer. "I've got a favor to ask of you. Could you get your great-granddad on the phone for me without letting your Dad know?"

"Sure," Katie said. "I'm walking over to his house now. Why do you want to talk to him?"

"I can't get into it right now, but it's nothing for you to worry about. I'll only take a minute of his time."

Maddy could hear the girl explaining the call to Ralph Miller. In a moment, his deep voice came over the line.

"Surprised to hear from you, Maddy, but it's a pleasure," he said, always the gentleman.

"I know it's a difficult time," she said, "but what I'm calling about is kind of urgent."

"What do you need? I'm happy to help if I can."

"My sister and I want to find out more about the feud between Albert Benson and your family. Can we come talk to you about it?"

"I guess. But why do you need to know?" Ralph asked. "Is my grandson in trouble over the argument he and Albert had at the rodeo?"

Maddy knew better than to soft-pedal the facts to the older man. "You know the police. They view everyone as suspects until they prove otherwise.

"The problem is, the homicide detective in charge appears to be mounting a case against Scott. The detective is a friend of mine, so I know how he operates. I don't want him to latch onto your grandson as a suspect. He'll be like a bulldog with a piece of mailman between his teeth."

There was no response. Maddy feared she had offended the man by being frank.

After a moment, he responded with a trace of amusement in his voice. "I agree, we don't want that to happen, but I have a better idea. I'll arrange for you and your sister to talk with someone who will be less biased than I might be. My version of things could seem too weighted in my grandson's favor to be of much help."

Maddy admired the man's willingness to expose the facts in the face of what could be perilous revelations. "I appreciate your candor. Who are you setting us up with?"

"A man who knows everything about our family history and someone who is known to speak the truth. He'll tell you the whole story. You can draw your own conclusions."

Chapter Three

The next day, Tom was on the road early enough to see silhouettes of surfers catching the first waves of the morning.

Much of the acreage to the south of town, originally citrus groves and strawberry fields, had been replaced by housing and retail centers. Tom's destination was an agricultural area northeast of Buena Viaje where all the large ranches and smaller farms were located. He turned off the freeway and headed inland.

The first item on his agenda was to interview the victim's immediate family: his nineteen-year-old son, Dalton, and Lucy, the twelve-year-old daughter he met at the scene of the murder.

He'd placed a call earlier to the victim's only known sibling, a brother in Kansas who had seemed unperturbed by the news of the sudden death. The man's only comment before hanging up was "With Albert's foul mouth and bad temper, it's surprising someone didn't pop him years ago."

Passing the Miller ranch, the largest and most well-known spread in the county, Tom drove through the gates of the adjacent property, the farm where Albert Benson had lived.

Weeds were overrunning the fields. The orchards were old, rotting, and unattended; only a few trees bore fruit. The ranch house and barn were in a run-down state, which required more extensive repair than a few cans of paint would provide. The vegetables in the garden were dry and shriveled as though under siege by insects.

The door was answered by a lanky kid of average height with wavy brown hair and blue eyes.

"You must be Dalton. I'm Detective Elliot. I met your sister yesterday at the rodeo."

"Lucy told me the cops would be coming to see us. She's not here. We stayed with the Millers last night. She's still over there. I had chores to tend to." His manner was serious, like someone who'd had a lot of responsibility from a young age.

"Mind if I come in?"

"Okay." He motioned for Tom to enter, swinging the door open awkwardly, and then rushed to clear empty soda cans from the couch, making room for Tom to sit.

"I'm sorry about your father, son. That's rough."

"We'll get by. I've been through hard stuff before."

"Like losing your mother?"

Dalton didn't reply. His head dropped, and he stared down at his folded hands.

Tom glanced around the room, noting the framed photographs above the fireplace. He stood to get a closer look.

There were several photos of the entire family. They were all of average stature and slight build. It was obvious Lucy had inherited her father's sunken eyes and pallid complexion. Dalton, on the other hand, was clearly the beneficiary of his mother's good looks.

Tom picked up a picture. "Is this you with your mother?"

Not surprisingly, the dazzling smile and dimples the boy displayed in the picture were now missing, but there was no denying the resemblance between Dalton and the striking woman. The young man could pass for a model except for the calloused hands and broken nails indicative of hard work.

"Yeah, that was my mom," the boy said, his voice flat.

"Do you remember much about her?"

"I remember everything," Dalton said, staring at the picture Tom replaced on the mantel. "I was the only child for seven years. The three of us did everything together: camping, fishing, hiking, mountain biking. We spent most of our time outdoors.

"My mother was an artist. She painted landscapes. Some Sundays, we'd visit the local galleries and Mom's pictures would be hanging there. Dad was really proud of her."

His face became more animated, and his eyes lit up. "Dad called me a mamma's boy, but in a loving way. I had the same eye for nature, but instead of painting, I captured it with my camera. I wanted to be a photographer when I grew up.

"Dad would laugh when I'd take my camera with me to feed the chickens or milk the cows. He'd tell me, 'You need to be chasing those rabbits away from our crops, Son, instead of trying to take their picture nibbling the lettuce.' But he was never really mad." His smile faded. "Back then."

"Did your father change after your mother died?"

"In a big way. I was hoping the baby Mom left us would help ease the pain. But the price he paid for my little sister was too much for him. He and I stopped doing fun stuff together. All we had time for was taking care of the newborn and the farm.

"The last picture I took was at my mother's funeral. I came home and stored my camera in a shoe box in the closet. I haven't snapped a shot since. The father I had my first seven years disappeared along with my mother and my dreams of being a photographer."

Tom felt for the boy. The young man was not as fragile as he appeared. Through his experience, he'd developed a maturity beyond his years.

"Did your father get over your mom's passing?"

"His grief faded, if that's what you're asking. But another side of him came out, a side I'd never seen."

"How so?"

"He got mean—not to the baby and me, but to other people. He seemed to resent their sympathy. When friends came to visit, he'd get touchy, like seeing them with their families reminded him of the kind of happiness he'd never have again."

"Did he get into any physical altercations?"

"He was known to throw a punch when he got drunk."

"How often did he get drunk?"

"He tried to stay away from the house when he was drinking for Lucy's sake, so I don't rightly know. But there were nights he didn't come home at all."

Tom didn't want to hurt the kid, but he needed to know what had been going on in the dead man's life. "Maybe your father found a woman friend."

Dalton's eyes blazed. "The day after my mother passed, he told me there would never be another woman in his life. It's the only promise he kept."

It was time to change the drift of the conversation. "I missed seeing you at the rodeo, but I'm glad you were able to avoid the scene."

"I should have been there for Lucy." He punched a pillow.

"Where were you?"

"I only go to competitions to help Dad and Lucy get ready. The rodeo's not my thing. I came back here to feed the cows."

"What will you and Lucy do now that your father's gone? Are there family members on your mother's side you can go live with?"

"Naw. I have an uncle back east, but he and Dad had a blowout. We haven't heard from him for years.

"It doesn't matter. I'll take care of Lucy. We'll sell this place. It's probably not worth much, but with some work, someone can make a decent living from it. Lucy and I will get an apartment in town. She'll be closer to her friends at school, and I can attend junior college. I finished one semester by taking night classes. I need to get my degree."

"So you're not interested in being a rancher like your father?"

"Not hardly. As far as I'm concerned, the only good thing about working on a ranch is being outdoors. I'm planning to be a forest ranger."

"That's an admirable goal. They can use all the help they can get taking care of natural resources."

Tom was reluctant to discourage the young man's plans, but from the condition of the property, selling could prove difficult. "The real estate market's in a slump, son. You may have a hard time finding a buyer."

"There's been interest recently. I think we'll do all right."

Tom sat back a moment before proceeding to the difficult part of the interview. "I'm anxious to find out who's responsible for your father's death, Dalton. I know this is painful to talk about, but do you have any idea who might have shot him? Did he have disputes with the other ranchers? Did he get in any arguments recently? Was he having money problems with the ranch?"

"There was hardly a week went by when he didn't get into an argument with someone," Dalton said, angrily. "That's the kind of person he was."

The boy hesitated, as his eyes clouded. "At least, that's the kind of person he's been ever since my mom died."

"Is there anyone in particular your father didn't like?"

Dalton hesitated again before dropping his head and shaking it. "Not really. He was an equal-opportunity guy when it came to people he disliked."

Tom sensed he wasn't getting the whole truth from Dalton but felt it fruitless to pursue the topic. He stood, reaching to shake hands. "Thanks for your help. I'll be in touch if I need anything else."

"Are you going to see Lucy now?" Dalton asked.

"That's where I'm headed."

"Take it easy on her, okay? She's pretty shook up."

"I understand. I got most of what I needed from her yesterday. I only have a few more questions." Tom turned before going out the door. "Do you and Lucy spend a lot of time at the Millers' ranch?"

"Lucy's close friends with Katie. I work for the Millers a couple of hours every day."

"I didn't realize that. Is that on top of helping out on your father's ranch?"

"Dad never paid me or gave me an allowance. He said it's a man's responsibility; part of being a man is taking care of your spread and your family. But I needed money for tuition and books. The Millers paid me enough to cover my school expenses. They probably paid me more than they should, but they kept telling me how important it was for me to get my degree so I could make choices about what to do with my life."

"It was good advice they gave you. They sound like generous people."

"They are. Generous and kind. Kinder to me than my father was."

* * *

Tom's next stop was the Miller ranch. The detective had done his homework as he always did before an interview. He knew the ranch was composed of more than fifty-thousand acres, with twelve-thousand head of cattle, forty acres of fruit orchards, twenty acres of vegetable crops, and an additional fourteen-hundred acres devoted to vineyards.

As he approached the stone columns at the entrance, an iron gate inlaid with the letter M swung open.

The disparity between the two homesteads was apparent not only in size but in appearance.

Pastures here were cross-fenced to separate grazing sheep and cattle. Several saddled horses were corralled, others roamed freely, lying under shade trees or frolicking in the pastures. Men walked in and out through the doors of a huge steel-beamed barn. Dust clouds trailed behind tractors and harvesters driven by workers wearing overalls and straw hats.

Parking his car on the paved driveway, Tom was greeted with the sounds of a bustling ranch: dogs barking, people calling out, engines humming. A far cry from the dull silence of the Benson place.

Walking through the wood-carved doors of the lodge, he was met by a gentleman with white hair and bushy white eyebrows who stood tall and sturdy like a towering oak.

"Good morning," the detective said, extending his hand. "Lieutenant Tom Elliot, Buena Viaje Police Department."

"Welcome. Ralph Miller," the older man reciprocated. "Nice to meet you. Haven't seen you out here before."

"I'm with the Homicide Division. I'm here investigating a murder that took place in town," Tom said. "I'd like to speak with Scott if he's available. He's expecting me."

"My grandson is checking on the herd with our foreman. He should be back momentarily. Can I offer you some coffee while you're waiting? Maria is brewing up a chicory blend that's mighty tasty. Guaranteed to get your blood moving."

The warm hospitality of the gentleman was a welcome relief from the reception Tom was accustomed to receiving. "I could use a jump start. I had a late night."

"I heard. The nasty business at the rodeo."

Ralph called out for his housekeeper, and the men settled into comfortable leather chairs.

"Scott told me about it before he brought the Benson kids over to spend the night. I'm sure my grandson will cooperate in any way he can."

Tom looked around the spacious room, surveying the stuffed animal heads on the walls. "From what I've heard, your grandson wasn't part of the ranch for some years."

"The ranch is a family tradition, passed down to me from my father. At one time, we had three generations working the land. Unfortunately, Scott and I had a parting of ways when he was in his early twenties."

"May I ask the cause of your falling out?"

"He experienced the common yearnings of a young man wanting to prove himself, get out on his own, become his own man. He felt he couldn't do it while he was still under the same roof with his father and me. He left and went to Colorado where he started a small spread of his own."

The housekeeper brought a tray and poured two cups of coffee before she left. Ralph leaned across the table to pass the cream and sugar.

"I thought Scott would come back when his father had a stroke a few years later, but Scott was resolute in his determination to be his own man. By that time, he was also married with a daughter. He came for the funeral but returned to his family in Colorado a few days later."

"What brought him back permanently?"

"I kept hoping Scott would return of his own volition, but it ended up being a tragedy that brought him back to us."

Ralph paused, crow's-feet forming around his eyes. "Scott's wife was killed in an automobile accident. He decided family would help him to get over the loss, and to raise his five-year-old daughter."

"I'm sure Scott and Katie's presence has meant a lot these past years."

"Their being here has meant the world to me." A smile spread across the man's face, making him look ten years younger. "Not wanting to miss a moment of Katie's childhood; that's what keeps me going."

Tom enjoyed listening to the older man. He had a way of sharing his life that made a person feel as though they'd known him for a long time.

The housekeeper came in with a plate of muffins. "Your favorite, Mr. Miller. Hot from the oven."

The smell of blueberries got Tom's salivary glands working. He took one from the plate Maria presented before Ralph objected. "Take two, Detective. You probably haven't had any breakfast."

"I haven't had time to think about food for the last forty-eight hours," Tom admitted. "It was nice of you to keep the Benson kids company last night since they have no immediate family in the area. I've just come from seeing Dalton."

"Then he probably told you he's here every day for a couple of hours," Ralph said.

"He told me the wages he gets from you pay his college tuition."

"He earns every penny, believe me. He's a hard worker."

"What about his father? From the looks of the Benson place, they're having a hard time of it."

"Albert's spread got away from him after he lost his wife. His heart turned cold enough to hang meat. He became a bitter, ornery man, making life miserable for whoever he could."

"Payback for his own misery?"

"I suppose," Ralph said, shaking his head. "We all have our way of handling the pain life doles out. I'd have to say Albert let his suffering get the better of him. It's not what Victoria would have wanted, especially for their kids."

"Do you know of anyone Albert's orneriness might have made angry enough to kill him?"

"I couldn't say. I don't know who he crossed paths with. When he wasn't stepping on someone's toes, he stayed pretty much to himself."

"When Dalton came over to work for you, did he ever mention his father being in trouble of any kind?"

"No, but that boy keeps personal stuff to himself. He's not a complainer. If his father were in any trouble, Dalton never let on to us about it."

Voices on the veranda caused both men to look to the front door where two men entered, shaking the dust from their gloves and hats. "Finish rounding up the rest of the cows. I'll be at the barn shortly to help with the ear tagging."

The other man walked away, and Scott joined the men in the room, shaking hands with Tom before pouring himself a cup of coffee and settling into an easy chair.

"How's the herd; any problems?" the older man asked his grandson.

"Nope. The cows are calm now, but they'll get riled up once we start putting tags on them."

Tom squirmed. "Sounds painful."

"Not really," Scott said. "Not much different than a person getting their ears pierced."

"That's not something I'd have the guts for either," Tom said, causing all three men to laugh.

Ralph stood up. "I'll let you two get to it. I've got my own work to do. Glad to meet you, Detective. Come out to one of our barbecues when you're not working. We'll give you a proper feeding."

"I'd like that. I've heard about your barbecues." The words slipped out before Tom caught Scott's expression.

"You've got an open invitation." Ralph smiled over his shoulder as he walked out. "Come anytime."

The two men left in the room glared at each other.

* * *

The men sat across from each other, Scott with his legs sprawled out and his arms resting on a cushioned chair. Tom wondered if he should have summoned Scott to police headquarters where the witness might not have felt so comfortable, but he doubted if surroundings would make a difference. The cowboy had an air that suggested he'd feel at home no matter where he was.

31

The detective decided to take a less aggressive approach. "Thanks for taking the time to see me. I realize you're a busy man overseeing a spread this size."

"It keeps me out of trouble." Scott's smile fell somewhere between friendliness and amusement.

"How did Benson's kids handle things? Dalton mentioned he and his sister spent the night with your family."

"Yeah. I brought Lucy straight here from the fairgrounds. I found Dalton at the Benson place. I told him to stay the night with us, and we'd sort everything out this morning."

"He was alone at his house when I met him this morning."

"He's an independent kid. I offered to accompany him, but he insisted he'd take care of things on his own. I figured he needed time alone to grieve."

"I've seen a lot of people experience grief in my job. He didn't fit the usual mold."

"He's not the usual kid."

"Let's get back to your squabble with Benson at the rodeo. What was that about?"

"It didn't amount to much. Albert was acting like a jackass, not unusual behavior for him. Saying things about my daughter I didn't appreciate."

"Any truth to what he was saying?"

"None."

"Is that what made you throw a punch?"

"A man can criticize me all he wants, rolls off like water on a duck. Say something derogatory about my daughter, we got a whole different situation on our hands."

"Was it the first time you two engaged in fisticuffs?"

"It happened once before at a meeting of the Cattlemen's Association. He'd been drinking before he came to the meeting. He got belligerent with me and several other ranchers. He accused us of conspiring against him."

"Conspiring how?"

"He had some wild notion everyone was out to take his land away from him. Accused people of poisoning his livestock and crops so he'd be forced to sell. Ended up by taking a swing at me. I refused to fight him in his condition. A couple of members grabbed his arms and escorted him from the building. He was barred from the association for disorderly conduct."

"From the looks of his crops, there could be some validity to his story."

"I went over there the next day and suggested that he get some tests done to figure out if his cows or crops were being poisoned. Even offered to pay for the tests."

"That was generous. Did it stem from a sense of guilt?"

Scott's lips thinned, but the corners of his mouth turned into a smile. "It stemmed from wanting to make sure it got controlled so it didn't happen to my herd."

"What were the findings?"

"Albert refused to have any testing done. I think he didn't want to be proved wrong and made to look like a paranoid fool."

"Is that what you thought—that he was a paranoid fool?"

"I paid him no further heed. If a man's not willing to back up the things that spew out of his mouth, he should shut up and get about his business."

A man entered the lodge, removing his hat and wiping sweat from his brow. He moved quickly toward Scott. "Boss, we got a problem."

Scott nodded in Tom's direction, and the man stepped back.

"Sorry to interrupt. I didn't realize you were in a meeting."

"Tom Elliot, my foreman, Miguel Torres," Scott said, neglecting to state Tom's official capacity.

"Go ahead," Tom said, standing to stretch his legs and walking toward a window. "We could use a break."

Miguel turned to his employer, twisting the band on his hat as he talked. "The stream on the back forty was blocked again this morning. This time, instead of the water being diverted off the property, it was directed toward the strawberry fields. Flooded more than half the berries before the hands discovered it." The man lowered his head as though taking responsibility for the ruined crop.

Scott walked Miguel to the door, putting his arm around the man's shoulders. "It's okay, Miguel; don't worry. Have the men salvage what they can. We'll let the fields dry out and replant. I'll be there shortly to look at the stream. We'll figure out how to dig a trench so it won't be so easy to divert."

Tom admired the easy way Scott had with his foreman. It made him reflect on his own management style. But resuming his seat, Tom noted lines furrowing across Scott's forehead.

"I'm no expert, but aren't there regulations about diverting water from a stream?" Tom asked.

"Some people get touchy if they think their neighbor is channeling water off their property. There was an occasion where a contractor wanted to pipe water from an adjacent water source without checking with the farmer and authorities to make sure they were okay with it. He and his client got fined. We tend to leave it up to the NRCS to determine if someone's overstepped their rights."

"The NRCS?"

"Natural Resources Conservation Service. Most of the rivers and creeks in this area are named on maps and visible from the county's aerial photos. The agency can determine fairly easily if someone's infringing on water access."

"Maybe it was more than an infringement on water rights. Benson said people at the Cattlemen's Association were forcing him to sell. Was there any basis for his accusation?"

"His claims were ludicrous."

"How can you be so sure? It sounds like you're experiencing some of the same problems."

"Having one field of strawberries ruined is hardly a threat to put us out of business. It only affected a couple of acres."

"Still, it sounds like it was an intentional act on someone's part. Perhaps the same person responsible for vandalizing Benson's property."

"Albert Benson's spread isn't worth enough to interest anyone in taking those kinds of radical measures."

"But surely, the Miller ranch is incentive enough for someone to be willing to take such measures. Have you had any other acts of sabotage?"

Tom noted Scott's hesitation, certain he was deciding how much information to disclose.

"First of all," Scott responded testily, "I don't know if the damming of the stream was deliberate. Second, it happened on an isolated part of the ranch that doesn't have much impact on the big picture. It's a piece next to Benson's property."

"Maybe someone was interested in scoring that piece and putting it together with Benson's farm."

Scott's hand moved up to his face, and he stroked his chin. "Some weeks ago, Gramps told me about someone expressing an interest in buying some acreage."

"Did your grandfather consider selling?" Tom asked.

"Gramps will never sell any portion of the land. He declined the offer like every other offer he's received over the years."

"Who made the offer?"

"As I recall, some young man presented it. Gramps wasn't interested enough to find out the source."

Scott twisted from side to side and looked at his watch. Tom assumed he was anxious to sort out his water issue.

"One last thing. Have you given any thought to who took the gun you couldn't produce for me at the fairgrounds?"

"I've given it a lot of thought, Detective," Scott said, his voice elevated by a sudden lack of patience. "I'm not naïve enough to think you won't attempt to use that gun to pin this murder on me. But I keep all my firearms locked, especially with a twelve-year-old daughter. I don't know who broke into the storage box. Did you get any fingerprints?"

"Not surprisingly, the gun was wiped clean. So I need to ask again. If you didn't fire the gun that killed Benson as you claim, who else had access to that gun?"

"Sorry, Lieutenant, I can't help you. I have no idea."

Scott's hesitation had lasted mere seconds, but long enough in Tom's mind to discount his response.

Chapter Four

Paul waited for his friend at Tommy's Burgers in midtown. The smell of grilling beef, bacon, and onions whetted his appetite. He ordered an appetizer and surveyed the selection of brews posted on the wall.

Tom slid into the booth across from him as the waitress set a plate of cheese fries on the table.

"How do you always manage to arrive the minute food is placed on the table?" Paul asked.

"It's a talent honed from growing up with two brothers," Tom said, stuffing fries into his mouth. "Bring me an iced tea and a double burger with bacon and mushrooms, please, Liz."

"Make mine the same," Paul said, folding his menu and handing it to the waitress.

"Sorry I missed the game yesterday," Tom said. "Did you guys manage to win without me?"

"Your replacement hit a home run with two on base in the bottom of the seventh. We won by one run. After that showing, you may be expendable."

Tom finished the last fry, licking ketchup from his mouth. "Never going to happen, buddy."

"I hear the reason for you missing the game was Albert Benson's murder at the rodeo."

"News travels fast. Guess I don't need to ask how you found out," Tom said.

Paul leaned back, eying the burger Liz placed in front of him. "What's my usual source for anything which smacks of murder and mayhem?"

"Lea and Maddy?"

"None other. Maddy couldn't wait to enlist my wife's help in defending her cowboy friend."

"Why in the sam hill is Maddy getting involved?" Tom asked.

"When did lack of good sense or reason prevent their sleuthing?" Paul shot back.

"She may actually have reason in this case."

"You mean her cowboy friend? Is there a reason he needs defending?"

Tom leaned back, reluctant to share details of a developing case, even with his closest friend. But he knew Paul was as opposed to the sisters' involvement in murder cases as he was. He doubted Paul would pass on to Lea any information they exchanged, and he needed Paul's help.

"His pistol is the murder weapon which places him pretty high on my suspect list, but I'm looking into other people with motives. That's why I offered to buy you a burger."

"I've never had a free meal from you yet," Paul said. "I didn't expect this was coming without a price."

"That's not true. Who's been paying the tab for our weekly foursome of wine-and-dine the last three weeks?"

"You've been paying off Lea's bet on who would solve your last case," Paul reminded him.

"I admit she was instrumental in solving the murder at the theatre," Tom said.

"It wasn't the first time she's made you look good," Paul jabbed.

"Do you want to help me, or waste my time giving your wife accolades?" Tom asked, wiping his mouth and throwing a wadded napkin on the empty plate.

"What do you need?"

"When I was interviewing Albert Benson's kid, Dalton, I asked him about his plans for their ranch. He told me he's going to sell it and use the money to take care of his sister, and to pay the expenses for him to finish college."

"Lofty plans, but his timing's not good. The real estate market is still slow."

"That's what I told him. He mentioned someone expressing interest in the property recently. When I asked for a name, Dalton said the person dealt with his father. He's hoping that person will contact him when he hears about the change of circumstances."

"I haven't heard anything about an offer made on Albert Benson's property," Paul said.

"There's more," Tom continued. "When I went to the Miller ranch, Scott told me his grandfather had been contacted by someone interested in buying a small parcel of their land."

"Two offers in a slow market," Paul said. "That sounds like more than a coincidence."

"I don't believe in coincidence," Tom said, "and the location of the Miller parcel is even more interesting; it's adjacent to Albert Benson's ranch."

"What about the neighbor on the other side?" Paul asked. "Was he contacted as well?"

"I'm going to see him after lunch; I'll let you know."

"Did Scott tell you who the interested party was?"

"He didn't know," Tom replied. "The offer came through an associate who kept his client's identity confidential."

"I'm not sure how I can help," Paul said.

"My thinking is the mystery party is not someone interested in buying a ranch; it's someone interested in buying land."

"You mean, like a real estate developer?" Paul asked.

"Bingo, and who knows more about developers in the county than you?" Tom said, referring to Paul's business as a consultant to real estate developers. "And what about builders? They buy land, too, right?"

"Are you clear about the difference between developers and builders?" Paul asked.

"Developers develop, and builders build, but developers make more money, right?"

"It depends," Paul answered, smiling. "A developer takes raw land, obtains the necessary permits, and divides the land into lots. He brings in sewer, water, and electric lines, and builds streets and curbs. Then the builder comes in and erects the houses.

"A builder can also be a developer; in fact, many are, but building and developing are two distinct and different tasks. Typically, most of the larger housing companies buy finished lots, or pads, from someone else."

"Are you saying someone buying up multiple parcels is more likely to be a developer?" Tom asked.

"It sounds like it."

"Good, that narrows my search. Do you think you could tap into your grapevine and find out who's planning a development in that area?"

"I think you're referring to my contacts at the Planning Department," Paul said.

"I have no basis for a warrant at this stage of the investigation," Tom admitted, "but I'd like to know who's interested in buying land in that neck of the woods."

"I'll see what I can do, but I may have less than a warm reception after my last foray into City Hall to get information for you."

"Are you kidding! You're probably a hero to those people after exposing the corrupt director in the Planning Department."

"We'll never know if it was my probing into misconduct or Lea's discovery of his relationship with the former Councilwoman which instigated his decision to resign, but I guess I'm about to test my popularity at City Hall."

"While you're at it," Tom added, "find out if anyone's done any testing for soil or groundwater contamination in that area. The cows at the Benson ranch were looking a mite peaked when I was there, and the crops were drooping more than a hound-dog's ears."

"Anything else I can do for you?" Paul asked with a sarcastic tone.

Tom stood to leave. "Nope; that's it. I appreciate it, man. I owe you."

Paul pushed the ticket in Tom's hand. "Start by paying the tab on your way out. You invited me to lunch, remember?"

* * *

Tom turned his vehicle into the driveway of the other property adjacent to Albert Benson's farm. From the county maps he had studied prior to his visit, the detective knew that the Hudson ranch surrounded the Benson farm in an L-shaped pattern, and that both properties had frontage on the dirt road parallel to the freeway.

Two farm dogs raced toward his car as he parked beneath the shade of a large oak tree. He petted the dogs when he got out of his car, and looked around as he walked toward the house.

The bright blue color on the roof of the barn matched the blue trim around the farmhouse. Trailers beside the barn were filled to the brim with ripe tomatoes and melons. The metallic clacking of grain being harvested could be heard. The smell of freshly-mown hay floated through the air.

Tom reached out his hand to a man wearing a John Deere baseball cap and overalls stretched across a protruding stomach. The rancher's only gesture of greeting was to nod without taking his hands out of his pockets. "You're the policeman who called."

"Tom Elliot, Mr. Hudson."

"You can call me Cliff, and no one calls me mister."

"From the looks of that produce," Tom said, nodding toward the trailers, "it looks like you're weathering the drought pretty well."

"We've got an on-site well. We've also got a rainwater storage system, but with the lack of rain the last several years, it hasn't been of much use."

"Your crops are in a lot better shape than those on Albert Benson's property. Do you attribute that to a better water supply?"

"I attribute that to superior farming skills. Albert Benson couldn't farm his way out of a pumpkin patch." The tone of Cliff's voice may have conveyed more harshness than he intended. "Let me retract my comment. Albert used to be a darned good farmer. Since his wife passed away, he's let everything slide. It's a shame to see his place so run down. It wouldn't be that way if my family still owned it."

A woman with an apron tied around her waist appeared at the doorway. "For heaven's sakes, Clifford; where are your manners? Invite the man in."

Her diminutive stature belied her imposing air. She leaned across her husband to grasp Tom's hand. "Mildred Hudson. Come inside; I've got a pitcher of sun-tea. How do you take it, sugar and lemon?"

"Lemon, please, ma`am," Tom said, following her into the house.

"There you go with the sir, ma`am stuff," Cliff muttered, bringing up the rear.

Taking a seat on the sofa, Tom noted the woman's touch in the furnishings: ruffled curtains, needlepoint pillows, and stained-glass lamps. He looked toward the recliner where Cliff settled in. "Your family owned the Benson ranch at one time?"

"A good piece of it." The farmer's tone was petulant. "Our original spread was almost five-hundred acres before it got cut down to its current configuration."

"What happened?" Tom asked.

"My grand-dad lost part of our ranch to Benson's grand-dad in a senseless poker game. He did everything he could to get it back, but no dice."

Tom smiled at Clifford's turn of phrase. "Why was it worth gambling over?"

"The parcel they wagered over is next to the river," Cliff said. "It gives whoever owns that land a direct water supply without the need for irrigation."

"I hope you're not rehashing that old piece of history," Mildred said, entering the living room with a tray and placing it on the table. Water drops ran down the side of the pitcher she lifted. Ice cubes clinked as she poured the tea, handing each man a glass.

"I didn't bring it up; the detective asked," Cliff said. He took a long swallow of the drink. "But, you have to admit, it's always made row farming more difficult without that piece to square the plot out."

"Our neighbor's been murdered, and here you are, talking poorly about his family," Mildred said, shaking her head. "I'm going out to do some gardening where I don't have to listen. Call me if you need anything."

"I assume you had no more luck than your grand-dad getting the land back from Benson," Tom said, after the woman left the room.

"I tried several years ago to no avail. Considering the condition the farm was in, I thought his refusal to sell was plain orneriness."

"Maybe his son will take over and put the place right," Tom suggested.

"Dalton's not interested in farming," Cliff said. "He'll sell now that his father's out of the picture."

Tom was surprised Hudson was aware of Dalton's intentions. "If the boy decides to bail, would you have an interest in acquiring the Benson land?"

"Hardly," Hudson replied. "I'm having trouble selling the land I got. Why would I want more?"

Tom's eyebrows arched. "You're trying to sell? You've got a nice operation here. Why get rid of it?"

"My land came out of Agricultural Preserve last year," Cliff replied.

Tom understood the reference to the county's program which encouraged farmers to continue agricultural use of their land instead of converting it to nonagricultural use by offering participating farmers a reduction in property taxes.

"Seems developers are enticing more and more of you farmers into selling your land when it expires from the Preserve," Tom said. "The impact in the county from conversion of farmland to residential and commercial use has been dramatic in recent years, and it's not always been favorable."

"You can't blame us for cashing in on all the hard work we've put in." Cliff's jaw stiffened, and his hands clutched the arms of the chair.

"Nobody's placing blame," Tom said. "Progress can't be stopped, but people don't realize that their endless supply of food is slowly disappearing."

"Don't worry; there are plenty of companies inventing synthetic food," Cliff said, an angry sneer on his face.

"I'm no health-food junkie," Tom said, "but the word synthetic when it comes to what I put in my mouth turns my stomach."

"I guarantee you're already consuming more artificial food than you're aware of."

"That's not a problem I care to think about."

"So what problem are you here about, Detective? I've got work of my own to do."

"Who do you know who might have had it in for Albert?"

"He pissed off a lot of people," Cliff said, "but I'm sure I'm not the only one telling you that."

"Can you narrow it down for me?"

The farmer leaned back and placed his hands on his knees. "Sorry, I can't help you."

The man's attitude was starting to irritate Tom. "How about you, did he ever tick you off?"

Cliff hesitated, weighing his response. "One time in particular, I recall. I had the roof on my barn replaced, something Albert should have done to his own barn. While the roofer was at it, I had him build out a loft. Albert heard the contractor's bulldozer and called the city to report illegal building activity."

"Did you confront him?"

"Nope; he was more of a nuisance than a threat," Cliff said. "I had the proper permits. I didn't waste time defending my actions to him."

"You mentioned being interested in selling. It won't be easy to do with the real estate market in a slump. Where do you intend to find prospective buyers?" Tom asked. "Have you listed your property with a broker?"

"I'm not unaware of market conditions, but no, the property's not listed," Cliff replied. "Actually, I wasn't thinking of selling until I was contacted last month by someone interested in acquiring land out here."

"That's interesting. Dalton Benson mentioned recent interest in their property. Do you know if it was the same party who approached you both about selling?"

"I doubt there's more than one entity interested in buying up chunks of ranch land."

Cliff's sarcastic tone grated on Tom. He ignored the farmer's attitude and continued his questions. "Can I ask the name of the party who made the offer?"

"You can ask, but I can't tell you." Hudson started sucking on a toothpick he pulled from his pocket. "It wasn't an offer in writing. It was a young fellow asking questions on behalf of some money guy. He didn't give the name of his client."

"Did you indicate that you'd be willing to sell?"

"I sure did. I wasn't about to pass up an opportunity to get out from under." The farmer leaned back in his chair. "I'm not opposed to spending the rest of my days rocking in a chair or throwing darts at the local tavern."

"But you didn't get a written contract?"

"The man made it clear that any offer would be contingent on their ability to acquire enough land."

"Did he indicate how much land the investor needed?" Tom asked.

"He was talking in the neighborhood of five-hundred acres."

"Wow! That's a significant amount of land."

"Yep, you can grow a lot of corn on a chunk of dirt that big." A smirk spread across Hudson's face. "But I doubt it's corn they're interested in growing."

"More like a subdivision is my guess," Tom said.

"I reckon."

"How big is your place?" Tom asked. "How much additional land were they looking at acquiring?"

"They told me exactly what they needed in order to make me a viable offer. My place, the Benson farm, and a strip on the Miller ranch that the river flows through."

Tom knew the answer to his next question, but he wanted to hear Cliff's response. "If Albert Benson received similar inquiries, do you know how he responded?"

"Like I said about the Bensons: we got a history. It wasn't the first time a Benson screwed a Hudson."

"Are you saying Albert refused to sell?" Tom asked. "That must have thrown a wrench in your plans."

"I didn't say my deal was screwed, but if it had been up to Albert, it would have been. Thankfully, the young fellow I talked with appears to be as enterprising as I am willing."

"What do you—"

"You've wasted enough of my time," Cliff said, spitting out a sliver of chewed toothpick. "I'm sure you can find your way out."

Tom walked through the screen door and saw Mildred Hudson planting irises in a flower box. "Mighty pretty posies, Mrs. Hudson. You've got a green thumb."

"Why, thank you, Detective," she said. "You can hardly be a farmer's wife without one."

Contrary to her professing no interest in their conversation, she had been in a position to overhear every word.

Chapter Five

Paul had time before his next meeting so he headed to City Hall hoping the Director of Planning would be available to speak with him. He anticipated that any questions of a specific nature would go unanswered on the basis of confidentiality so he adopted a posture of seeking information for a proposed housing development on the outskirts of town.

After parking in the public lot, he climbed the wide sweeping stairway that led to the entrance of the government building. He walked under the ornate archway and down a long hallway decorated with imposing pictures of past dignitaries.

The woman at the front desk of the Planning Department greeted him with a friendly smile.

"How you doing, Mr. Austin?" she asked. "Long time, no see."

"Hey, Birdie. How's your son doing at the university; has he graduated yet?"

"He sure did. Now he's got the daunting task of finding employment, which can't come too soon for me. What can I help you with?"

"Any chance of my bending the director's ear for a moment?"

"He's in his office, let me find out. May I tell him the nature of your business?"

Paul crossed his fingers behind his back and presented the story he had concocted.

"Give me a minute," Birdie told him. "I'll see what I can do."

Paul took a seat. He had yet to meet the new Planning Director; helping Tom was giving him an excuse for an introduction.

Birdie returned a moment later. "He has time to see you. Go on back to his office."

* * *

After congratulating the director on his new position and exchanging pleasantries, the two men got down to business.

"Birdie mentioned you'd like a read on how favorable the city might be toward a new project your client is considering."

"That's right. He's asked me to evaluate a potential land purchase. I'm trying to save him the time and money of a feasibility study by determining whether a subdivision can be done, or at least done in a way which makes financial sense."

The director nodded. "Always better to perform adequate due diligence before a substantial sum of money is invested. What's the location and scope of the plans?"

Paul responded with a generic description. "One to two acres per lot, fifteen or twenty lots, on the east side of the river. Ideally, land which fronts on a public road."

The director leaned forward over his desk. "As long as your client is amenable to bringing necessary infrastructure to the property, he should have no problem winning the Council's approval. In a robust economy, he'd have more red tape to go through, but the Council is pro-growth right now due to loss of tax revenue."

"Are you aware of any environmental concerns?"

"It depends on the location," the director answered. "Of course, your client will need to have an Environmental Impact Report done when they get to that stage of the planning. Overall, the few issues we hear complaints about are water access due to the drought, Indian burial grounds, and endangered bird species. I'm sure you've had experience with all those issues."

"More experience than I care to remember," Paul said.

"Stop by Birdie's desk on your way out to read the public reports on the land your client is considering. The Public Works Department will give you information on mineral and water rights. But short of talking about specific acreage, I can assure you the city will be proactive where new development is concerned."

"That's good to hear. Thank you for your time," Paul said, standing to leave.

"Not at all," the director said. "Those are the same answers I gave the fellow who was in my office last month asking the same questions."

* * *

Paul stopped at the front desk as the director had advised. "Birdie, I'd like to check the zoning and parcel ownership of some land east of town."

"Sure, Mr. Austin," she said, placing an open book in front of him. "Write down the address or the parcel numbers you're interested in, and sign the register. I'll bring out the corresponding plat maps for you to examine."

Paul didn't hear her final comment. His attention was riveted to the signature of the last person to request information on the Benson, Hudson, and Miller parcels.

"Something wrong, Mr. Austin?" Birdie asked.

"I see my client's associate has been here ahead of me. I won't need those plat maps after all."

As soon as Paul reached his car, he wasted no time calling Jim Mitchell's office.

"Jim's at the condominium site on Wheeler Road," the receptionist told him. "You can find him there."

"It's on the way to my office," Paul said. "I'll drop by."

* * *

As he got closer to his destination, his progress was impaired by large trailers hauling construction materials. Driving through the gates of a fenced property, Paul was struck by the sights and sounds of buildings being raised from the dirt, a beehive of activity that got Paul's blood pulsing.

He parked in front of a large trailer at the entrance which displayed the name of the project and a sign with the wording 'Opening Soon'. Stepping from his car, he was immersed in the noisy clamor of hammering and welding, the warning beeps of construction vehicles backing up, and laborers hollering to be heard. It was all music to his ears.

He walked through the door and waved to a tall man bending over a table which displayed a model of the project.

Jim Mitchell walked toward Paul, extending his hand. "Hey, Paul. Good to see you. What are you doing out here in the trenches?"

"I was in the neighborhood," Paul said. "You know I can never resist an opportunity to visit a construction site. This one's moving right along."

"Yeah, this is turning out to be a sweet project. Knock on wood, but so far we're ahead of schedule and under budget. Grab a chair. We've got a pot of the usual construction-site sludge brewing around here somewhere."

"No thanks; I'm good. Actually, I had you on the brain from my visit to City Hall this afternoon."

"What made you think of me?" Jim asked.

"I was gathering information for another client and saw your associate's name, Mike Young, on the register to review parcel data."

The developer reflected a moment before responding. "I don't recall sending Mike to City Hall for anything lately, but we've got several projects in the fire. He may have been checking on permits."

"He was looking up information on property owners. Do you have any acquisitions in the pipeline?"

"Not really. A month or so ago, a corporate investor expressed interest in doing a residential project outside of town, but we ran into some early hurdles and their interest waned. It would have been a good-sized project. I was sorry we couldn't proceed."

"Where was the proposed location?"

"They were looking at five hundred acres east of town. The concept was to subdivide into two- or three-acre parcels and build ranch-style houses. Each parcel would be big enough for people to grow their own crops."

"You mean a live-off-the-land concept?"

"More or less. The eco-friendly, living-green notion which is so popular."

"What were the hurdles you mentioned?"

"We weren't able to buy the amount of land needed. My associate made inquiries on three adjoining properties. One rancher was eager to sell. Apparently, he's close to foreclosure. If he can't sell, the bank will take his ranch. Unfortunately for him, the offer depended on all three properties being purchased."

"The other two ranchers weren't interested in selling?"

"No, my associate couldn't come to terms with either of them. We tabled the project. I didn't hear anymore about it." Jim's eyes narrowed as he scanned Paul's face. "What's your interest?"

"No specific interest. I like to get a read from anyone who's submitting building plans to the city. As you know, the City Council's partiality changes from month-to-month. You never know when you'll get a green light from them. I try to prevent wasting my clients' time and money if I'm sure a project will never make it through preliminary plan approval."

"That's one of the reasons I hire you. You're always as judicious with my money as I am. Sorry I can't be more help, but feel free to talk to Mike if you like."

"Thanks, Jim. No need for me to take up anyone else's time," Paul said, making his way to the door. "Good to see you. Call me when you have time for a game of racquetball. I've been practicing, I may be able to give you a run for your money."

"I doubt that," Jim said, "but I'm up for the challenge. I'll give you a buzz."

Before returning to his office, Paul called to report his findings to Tom. "My visit to City Hall was unproductive. Someone had checked on the parcels out by the Benson farm, but when I ran down the lead, the developer informed me his client had dropped the project. They're not pursuing an acquisition. Real estate as a motive appears to be a dead-end."

"Au contraire," Tom said, sounding smug. "After our lunch, I went to see Cliff Hudson. From what he told me, I'd say a land deal is still on the table as a motive. Someone may be lying to you, buddy. Come by my office. I'd like to hear more about your client."

* * *

Lea was working on an employee handbook when she got an unexpected call. "Hey, babe, I thought you were in meetings this morning."

"I am, or I was," Paul sputtered. "I'm on my way to another appointment, but I need to see you. Can you meet me at Maria's?"

"The donut shop in the middle of the week? You don't usually indulge in pastries until Saturday morning. What's the occasion? Are we celebrating or commiserating?"

"Something has come up. I don't have time to come by the house, but I need your input."

"I'll be there in fifteen minutes," Lea agreed, pleased to be consulted.

"Please don't be late." The phone went dead.

"Something's wrong," Lea told the dogs. "Paul knows how punctual I am; he never reminds me to be on time. Let's go find out what's got him upset."

* * *

Lea inhaled the sickly sweet smell of globby dough being baked into jam-filled donuts.

"Hi, Maria," she greeted the owner. "Where's Paul? I saw his car in front."

"He's gone to the bank, he'll be right back. How are you?" Maria asked, walking around the counter to hug Lea and lean over the eager canines.

"Yes, I have something for you," she told them.

She reached for a canister labeled 'For Dogs Only'. Gracie and Spirit waited, tails wagging. Maria threw the biscuits on the floor, and watched the dogs gobble them up as Paul walked in.

"Two cups of espresso, Maria," Paul said, "and a croissant for my wife."

Lea raised her eyebrows as Maria turned to prepare the coffee. "That was abrupt. I don't even get to look at the goodies?"

"I don't have much time," he said. He steered her to a table. "Besides, you always end up ordering the same thing."

"What's going on?"

"I have to go see Tom at police headquarters." Paul explained the events which had transpired.

"Why does Tom want to see you?"

"When I told him profit from a land deal couldn't be a motive, he told me I was wrong."

"What reason did he give?"

"He talked with Albert Benson's neighbor, Cliff Hudson," Paul said. "Apparently, Hudson was reluctant to disclose it at first, but he eventually told Tom there was an offer in the works."

"I thought you said your client wasn't interested in buying the property."

"That's what my client led me to believe. Now, I'm not so sure."

"Jim Mitchell would never lie to you. There must be another explanation. The offer must be coming from some other developer."

"That's what I thought until I saw the name on the register at the Planning Department."

"Not Jim Mitchell, I hope."

"No, it wasn't Jim."

"Then why are you so worried?"

"It was Jim's associate, Mike Young. It looks like Mike may have contacted all three property owners. Two of them turned him down, but strange things have been happening since."

"Like what?"

"Like livestock and crops being poisoned."

"How terrible." Shock registered on Lea's face.

"I know. This whole thing has taken an ominous turn."

"But if Mike made offers to those ranchers," Lea asked, "why did Jim tell you his client wasn't pursuing an acquisition?"

"That's what I need to find out," Paul said. Lines burrowed across his forehead. "Once Tom finds out Jim had an investor lined up for a residential development which would net Jim a huge profit, he's going to consider my client a suspect."

"But you can tell Tom it was Mike Young who made the offer."

"It doesn't matter. Jim's responsible for the actions of his employees. Tom's never going to believe Mike wasn't acting on Jim's behalf."

"What did Jim say when you told him you'd be talking to the police?"

"I haven't told him yet," Paul said. He avoided his wife's stare by looking down at his coffee cup. "I have no doubt if I tell Jim about Tom's suspicions, he'll deny any knowledge."

"And you think that's the case?"

"Absolutely. I'd stake my reputation on the man's honesty. If he says he has no knowledge of offers proffered for the purchase of land, I believe him. The question is whether offers were presented without his knowledge and why. That's what I came to talk to you about."

"Me?" Lea's eyes widened. "How am I involved in all this?"

"You know the last thing in the world I want to do is involve you in a murder investigation—"

"I know your feelings on the subject all too well," Lea said, noting the pained expression on her husband's face. "Considering how many times you've told Maddy and me to keep our noses out of anything remotely related to crime, I'm finding your request for help more than surprising."

"It will only require a minimal level of involvement on your part, but your instincts about people are impeccable."

"You and Tom usually ridicule my woman's intuition, as you call it. Interesting," Lea continued, "how that same instinct turns into a valuable asset when you need help."

"Since Jim denies his company's involvement," Paul said, ignoring her rebuke, "I have no cause to approach Mike Young. I'm hoping you can initiate a conversation with Mike to determine if he's done something behind Jim's back."

Lea scrunched her shoulders. "What excuse would I have for talking with Mike? I've seen him at Jim's ground-breaking ceremonies, but I have no reason to request a meeting."

"Don't worry; I've worked it all out. I asked Jim if he would be open to your submitting a proposal for a grand-opening event and marketing materials for his condominium project. He was more than receptive to the idea. I suggested he make his associate available to provide the information you need. Mike Young is expecting your call to set up a meeting."

"You did all that without talking to me?" Lea said, dismayed.

Paul smiled seductively, and grasped her hand. "Are you telling me you're going to turn down the chance to get involved in a mystery?"

"No way," Lea beamed. "Especially not when I have your blessing."

* * *

Lea called Maddy at the furniture store. "Can you take a break? I need to talk to you about the Benson murder."

"Give me fifteen minutes, and meet me at the Starbucks down the street."

"I'll be there."

* * *

Lea was sitting at an outside table with a frothy latte in front of her when her sister arrived. "You won't believe what Paul has asked me to do."

"Charter a fishing boat?" Maddy suggested, alluding to Lea's previous narrow escape from drowning at the hands of a ruthless thug.

"Very funny," Lea said, blowing on her coffee. "He wants me to pursue a lead on a possible suspect."

"Now you're the one who's being funny. I don't believe you."

"It's true. He's worried one of his clients may come under suspicion. He wants me to uncover the truth before the man is falsely accused."

"Something Tom is totally capable of doing," Maddy quipped, still smarting over the innuendos Tom had made about Scott. "Who does he want you to check out, Sherlock?"

"An associate of Jim Mitchell's who's been making offers to buy up land around Albert Benson's property without his boss' knowledge."

Maddy reached over to scoop the whipped cream from Lea's drink. "That sounds interesting."

"Hey," Lea objected, "where are you going with that?"

Maddy popped the cream in her mouth and licked the spoon. "What does Paul think the associate is up to?"

"He's not sure," Lea said, "but he's worried that Jim Mitchell could be implicated even if Jim has no knowledge of his associate's actions."

"Why doesn't Paul handle it?"

"He doesn't want to get the employee in trouble with Jim if there's a good reason for his behavior," Lea said. "Besides, Paul has no plausible reason to question Mike."

"I assume that's where you enter the picture," Maddy said. "Not that you've ever needed a reason to snoop, but what cover have you come up with?"

"Paul's arranged a meeting for me to get information to submit a proposal for the advertising campaign on Jim's condominium project. I'm meeting with Mike Young tomorrow morning."

"You seem very pleased with yourself," Maddy said. She pinched her lips into a pout. "It was like pulling teeth to get you involved when it came to Scott. Paul asks for help, and you're all in."

"Don't be silly," Lea said, reaching across the table to grab her sister's hand. "Look at it this way: by finding the real killer, we'll take care of both your friend and Paul's client."

"Isn't there some kind of conflict in trying to prove two people innocent?"

"We aren't representing anyone," Lea insisted. "We're simply fact-finders, trying to make certain that justice is served."

"Yeah, whatever. The only service I'm interested in right now is having a slice of carrot cake delivered to our table."

"Get your mind off your stomach, and tell me what progress you've made on your end."

"I've set up a different kind of meeting," Maddy said. A smile like a Cheshire cat spread across her face. "You and I are going to pow-wow with an Indian chief to find out the cause of the ruckus among the ranchers."

"That sounds intriguing." Lea paused. "By the way, in case you talk to Tom, don't mention what I'm doing for Paul."

"Ditto our meet-up with the chief. No sense stirring up a hornet's nest."

Chapter Six

Lea's meeting with Mike Young was at the company's corporate office, within walking distance of the county government facilities. Mitchell Development Company occupied the top floor of a three-story office building tenanted by professional people.

As she waited for the associate to make an appearance, she considered the purpose of their meeting. She hated to admit to herself how important it was to accomplish the task Paul had assigned her.

For once, Paul was asking for her help in a capacity other than professional writing. He readily acknowledged that she had the skills and discipline necessary to produce employee handbooks and marketing material. The area he didn't give her credit for was her interest in crime.

He chalked up her passion for sleuthing to women's curiosity, or the investigative nature she inherited from her father, a former police captain. But to her, it was more than that. It was a fascination with human nature and the events in people's lives, together with their response to those events, which led to seemingly inescapable, and sometimes disastrous, outcomes.

Most of the time, she was content to stick with familiar routines, relying on past knowledge and experience, and staying within the bounds of what felt comfortable. But there were times she wanted to stretch her limits, exceed those sensible, safe boundaries, and push her intuitive skills to the maximum. Sleuthing with her sister provided that outlet.

Paul typically took little notice of her involvement in activities outside the contract work she did from home. When it came to her detecting, his tendency was to humor her rather than to take her seriously.

But this time he had come to her which meant there was less chance he would trivialize her findings. He might begin to visualize her more in a role of intuitive investigator rather than creative copywriter.

* * *

She tapped her shoe on the floor, flipping through outdated issues of Architectural Digest in the reception room. She knew the time she spent waiting for a meeting had a direct relation to the confidence level of the participants. Self-assured clients valued another person's time; they arrived at the appointed time. Others, with a need to impress people with how busy they were, arrived late.

A woman appeared who introduced herself as Helen Taylor, and led Lea to an inner office. She offered Lea a cup of coffee and said Mr. Young would be arriving shortly before returning to the work she was doing on her computer.

"Your boss must be having a busy day," Lea said, looking at her watch.

"Oh, he's busy all right," the woman said. Her lips thinned. "Between you and me, busy and productive are two different things."

Waiting suddenly got interesting for Lea. She looked more closely at Helen Taylor, a woman of middle-age wearing a tailored suit and a neck scarf, with her hair pulled back in a chignon. Her make-up was lightly but expertly applied. "How long have you been working for Mr. Young?"

"Thank heavens, I don't work for him. I work for Mr. Mitchell. I'm filling in, helping Mr. Young prepare a report my boss will be presenting at an investors' meeting tomorrow."

"Doesn't Mr. Young have an assistant of his own?"

"Not at the moment. He's gone through more assistants in the time he's been here than Mr. Mitchell's gone through his entire career." Her remarks were punctuated with a deep, throaty chuckle.

"He sounds difficult to work for," Lea said.

"Mike Young is an ambitious young man trying to make a reputation for himself. He lacks experience, but that will come with time.

What can't be learned by a person whose motives are dictated by money is a passion for the business, and the integrity to ensure it's done the right way."

The woman looked over the top of the reading glasses resting half-way down her nose. "I'll reserve further comment and simply say I feel privileged to work for Mr. Mitchell."

Lea saw the woman's candor as a way to get more information. "I'm preparing a bid to do the marketing on the condominium project. I've heard there's another residential project coming up. I'd like to submit a proposal for that, too. Is there any truth to the rumor?"

"You must be talking about the ranchette project east of town. It depends on who you talk to. Mr. Mitchell hasn't worked on it since initial offers were rejected, but yesterday, I heard Mike pitching the project to an investment banker. From the way Mike was talking, a person would think the whole project was his idea.

"In fact," Helen went on, "the initial concept came from Mr. Mitchell's client. If the development happens, Mike will only be one of several assistants helping Mr. Mitchell."

Voices were heard in the hallway. The woman returned to her work as a young man strode into the office casting an offhand comment in Lea's direction.

"Sorry to be late, busy day," he said. "Please, come in."

"No problem," Lea said, winking at Helen Taylor.

* * *

Lea observed Jim Mitchell's youngest associate as he removed a laptop from his briefcase. A man in his late-twenties, genes were most likely responsible for Mike Young's bald head. His well-muscled physique, row of perfectly-capped teeth, and tailored suit suggested that appearance was important to him. The trace of a southern accent flowed as smoothly as bourbon.

"I appreciate your making yourself available on short notice. I'm sure you have a full schedule," Lea said.

"I have my hand in a lot of pots," the young man agreed, "but I'm always here for whatever Jim needs. The condominium project is one of his favorites. We're anxious for it to receive a good launch. The grand-opening will be important in generating interest. We expect pre-sales to go well."

"Your accent suggests you aren't a native," Lea said.

"I grew up in Texas and attended business school out here on a scholarship. I met both Jim and my future wife at a beach party my roommate dragged me to. It turned out to be the best weekend of my life." He leaned back with a self-satisfied look. "I married her and went to work for him six months later."

"You're young to be an associate."

"I'm a goal-setter. I know exactly where I'm going. The day of graduation I wrote on a piece of paper how much money I'd have in my bank account on my thirtieth birthday. My birthday is two months away and I've almost reached that number."

"It sounds like you're handsomely compensated."

"My salary's more than adequate," Mike said, "but it's the profit-sharing I participate in on Jim's projects which sweetens the deal."

"How do you like working for Jim?"

"He's great; I've learned a lot from him. The only thing I could fault him on is coloring inside the lines a little too much for my liking. I'm the creative type, I like to think outside the box."

"What other projects have you worked on?"

Mike described several developments in the county from what Lea felt was a self-serving bias, attributing successes to personal efforts, and failures to factors beyond his control.

"It sounds like you're making a real name for yourself in the industry."

"That's my plan," he said. "Now, how can I help you with marketing material?"

* * *

They spent the next hour discussing the condominium project until Lea saw Mike look at his watch. She didn't want to leave without finding out what Paul needed to know. She sensed an appeal to the young man's vanity was her best approach.

"What new projects will you be dazzling us with once this present development is successfully launched?"

He stretched his arms behind his head and cradled his head in his hands. "I've convinced Jim the time is ripe to build some single-family ranchettes east of town. People are about self-survival now. They want to grow healthy food, live in clean air, and surround themselves with nature."

"That's quite an undertaking," Lea said. Helen Thomas was right; Mike made the project sound like his idea.

"It will be the biggest residential development folks around here have ever seen," Mike continued. "It will make Mitchell Development Company the most sought after developer in the county."

"That sounds wonderful. How many houses are you proposing?"

"It depends on how much land we get our hands on, and how the city allows us to subdivide the parcels. It could be anywhere from fifty to more than one-hundred dwellings."

"I didn't realize there was so much vacant land available."

"That's where thinking outside the box comes in," Mike boasted. "I've figured a way to parcel together land from existing farms."

"Aren't most of the farms and ranches still in Agricultural Preserve?"

"That's what makes finding the right number of contiguous parcels expired from the Preserve a once-in-a-lifetime opportunity."

"I'm surprised you find farmers willing to sell their land once the restriction is lifted. After all, they're giving up their livelihood, something they've spent a lifetime doing, in exchange for a specified amount of money."

"You're right. Many farmers aren't interested in selling, but most of them come around, given the right incentive."

"What kind of incentives do you offer?" Lea asked, trying to maintain a neutral tone.

"Whatever it takes to close the deal."

The smug look on Mike's face made Lea feel uncomfortable. She was relieved when he ended the meeting.

* * *

After leaving the meeting with Mike, Lea went into the coffee shop on the ground floor. Waiting at the front desk to be seated, she noticed Helen Taylor, the woman from Mike's office, seated in a booth by herself. The woman waved her over. "Why don't you join me? It gets crowded during the lunch hour."

"Thanks, I'd love to."

"The lunch special is good today," Helen suggested.

"Lunch special, it is," Lea told the waitress, "and iced tea, please."

"I hope your meeting with Mike was productive," Helen said after the waitress left.

"As productive as he wanted it to be. He spoon-fed me information in the exact wording he wants used in the marketing material. I'm not sure I understand why he's bothering to hire a marketing consultant at all."

"Because Mr. Mitchell wouldn't be satisfied with the presentation if it were left in Mike's hands. Even though Mike assumes he can do everything better than anyone else, Jim is smart enough to hire experts for each phase of the project. Mr. Mitchell will be best served if you sift through the information Mike gave you, and apply your professional skills to the marketing campaign."

The woman's directness appealed to Lea. "That's my intent," she assured her.

"With your looks, I was hoping Mike might proposition you to replace his last assistant so I could get back to my regular work for Jim."

"I wouldn't be interested in working for anyone, but Mike didn't make any suggestions."

"He probably lost interest after talking with you. He's easily threatened by any woman he thinks is smarter than he is."

Lea choked on her tea, and both women laughed.

"With all the equal opportunity floating around, he's more worried about a woman rising above him than a man," Helen said.

"He doesn't act like a person who's worried about anything, least of all, his own success. He made a point of assuring me he's well on his way to achieving his goals. He has the self-serving attitude I saw too much of when I worked in the corporate environment."

"I hear you," Helen said, cutting the crusts off her sandwich. "It's become 'forget the company: it's all about me.' Employees don't have much loyalty anymore."

"To be fair," Lea said, "companies don't stand by their employees the way they used to either."

"That's why I'm grateful to work for Jim. He views the company's business as a team effort, and makes sure his employees are rewarded accordingly."

"I don't mean to be unduly critical of Mike," Lea said, retracting her previous statement. "But his type reminds me of a boy I went to school with. He was good-looking and outgoing with the self-assurance that comes with being from a wealthy family. He excelled at everything, and won a lot of awards. He also had a big ego, and a tendency toward being a show-off. He could be a bully when he chose to be."

"Yes, I know the type."

"Our freshman year, this boy and I were elected from a group of ten nominees to serve on the student council. I couldn't imagine why I won.

"I have a sister who's a year older than me. Growing up, she was the extrovert; easy-going, popular, fun-loving. She knew everyone in our school by their first name. I was the shy, studious one who made our parents proud with good grades. I was surprised enough students even knew who I was to vote me onto the council.

"I dreaded our monthly lunch meetings. I'd get a stomach-ache the night before, worrying about what I should say. When the president of the council called on me, I was too tongue-tied to contribute anything. My counterpart always had stunningly, brilliant ideas for projects the school could undertake. I knew the brainstorms he took credit for came from his groupies.

"From that first year, he had visions of being president of the student council in our senior year. All I hoped for was that someone else would be elected in my place.

"I still get a knot in my stomach when I'm in the presence of someone with that kind of arrogance."

"We're all inclined to judge people based on personal experience," Helen said. She covered her glass as the waitress offered refills. "We have subconscious prejudices we aren't even aware of."

"I may have mistakenly reached the conclusion that Mike sets broad boundaries when it comes to what he will do to further his career, but it does make me wonder how far he's willing to go."

"What are you referring to?" Helen asked.

Lea leaned back while the waitress removed her empty plate. "When I asked about the ranchette development, he represented it as a viable project and was anxious to take credit for the progress being made. Am I wrong in reaching the conclusion from your earlier remarks that Mike is pursuing the project behind Jim's back without his boss' knowledge?"

"I can't say Jim has no knowledge of ongoing activity, but I can tell you that you haven't missed the mark in your assessment of Mike and how far he's willing to go. Your instincts about him are correct."

"Would he stoop to sabotage?"

"He wouldn't dirty his own hands," Helen said, "but that doesn't mean he wouldn't put a bug in someone else's ear to do it."

"Do you have anything specific in mind?" Lea asked, sensing that she was onto something.

"I overheard Mike telling someone on the phone they should do whatever was necessary to grab a once-in-a-lifetime opportunity," Helen said. She looked at her watch and stood to leave. "It's time for me to get back. I've enjoyed talking with you."

Lea picked up Helen's bill. "Let me get this."

"Thank you," Helen said. "Good luck with your submission."

Lined up at the cashier's desk, Lea noticed Mike Young in a booth at the front. All she saw of the man sitting across from him was the back of the man's head, but the overalls were an interesting contrast to Mike's pin-striped, tailored suit.

* * *

Lea returned to her car and called Paul with her impression of Jim's associate.

"I'm glad to hear from you," Paul said, anxiety flooding his voice. "I'm avoiding Tom, but he'll want answers when we get together for dinner tonight. How did your meeting go?"

"Mike gave no indication that the ranchette development isn't ongoing. He was more than happy to pat himself on the back and to tell me what a great thing it will be for Buena Viaje."

"Were you able to ask if his boss considers the project to be active?" Paul asked.

"I think I can safely say that Jim and his associate are at odds in their view of whether or not that project is on a go-forward basis."

"What about the damage to the ranchers' property? Was there any mention of that?"

Lea repeated Helen's comments about Mike's phone conversation with an unknown party.

"It sounds like Mike was playing on someone's baser instincts to encourage them to do whatever needed to be done in order for Mike to achieve his own ends," Paul said.

"Are you going to tell Jim what Mike said?"

"It's a sticky situation," Paul admitted. "I don't want to put Mike in a bad position with Jim, but I think Jim needs to know. What do you think?"

"I think Tom is the person who needs to know. As far as I'm concerned, he's looking at the wrong person in Jim's company as a suspect."

She sat in the parking lot wondering if she was guilty of jumping to conclusions about Jim Mitchell's associate the same way Tom was jumping to conclusions about Scott Miller. Were her personal past experiences and prejudices casting a shadow over an innocent man, or was Mike Young taking advantage of the only person who had showed an eagerness to sell?

Chapter Seven

When the officers of the Homicide Division gathered for their daily meeting, one of the men asked a question Tom had been avoiding since his return from vacation.

"Hey, Lieutenant," Jensen asked. "We aren't giving up on Operation Kingpin are we, just because that oily Card Club owner got away?"

The room went silent. Several officers shook their heads hearing the ill-advised question. All eyes turned to the man at the front of the room.

Tom's steely gaze zeroed in on the questioner like a laser honing in on its prey. "No, Jensen. We aren't giving up on Operation Kingpin."

The Kingpin was a racketeer linked to illegal gambling, drugs, and prostitution, but to the crime team's great frustration, all previous attempts to identify and indict the gangster had failed.

Tom was still smarting over the escape of Mickey Flynn, a bookie long suspected of fronting the Kingpin's gambling operation. The homicide team had hoped to file criminal charges against the bookie strong enough to convince him to give up his boss.

But the bookie had anticipated the danger. By putting an undercover officer's life at risk, Tom's hand had been forced before the sting operation could be brought to a successful conclusion. The owner of the Card Club was still on the lam, and Tom was no closer to the Kingpin, his ultimate target.

"But the next time we get our hands on someone who might roll over on the guy," Tom said, his voice as cold as steel, "I'm going to make sure they don't get away."

"Hold on, Lieutenant," the newest member of the homicide squad argued, stepping forward. "Are you implying I'm to blame for Mickey's escape?"

"Don't worry, Pat," Tom said. "No one here thinks you blew your cover. You did a great job, especially for a rookie, but Mickey Flynn was one step ahead of us. I won't let that happen again. Until we get the opportunity to make a fool-proof arrest, we're focusing on other cases."

Pat Fisher relaxed and stepped back. No one felt the disappointment of losing the man who might have brought down the Kingpin more than she did.

Tom had assured her she had nothing to prove to her fellow officers, but she knew she still wasn't accepted as a member of the team. She hoped the inside knowledge which only she and Tom shared would give her another opportunity to earn her stripes.

* * *

The officers dispersed after the meeting with the exception of Pat, who lingered behind at Tom's request.

"You and I both know what we need to do to make sure the Kingpin won't second-guess our next move," Tom said.

Pat knew what Tom was referring to. Before being taken hostage by Mickey Flynn in his bold escape, Pat had recorded a conversation in which Mickey had accused her of being the mole the Kingpin had planted in the Police Department. Hearing about a possible traitor on his team had been a shock to Tom, but it explained how the Kingpin had been able to anticipate the homicide squad's every move for the last year.

"You mean we have to find the snitch Mickey alluded to before he made his hasty departure," Pat said.

"Any new attempt to identify and arrest the Kingpin will be useless if we don't flush out the back-stabber." Tom's tone sounded unduly harsh.

"The Kingpin has really gotten under your skin, hasn't he, Lieutenant?"

"You bet he has. That scum is into every illegal activity there is. You name it, he's done it. He's been poisoning kids with drugs, ruining young women's lives by inducting them into his prostitution rings, and exploiting people's gambling addictions for over a decade in this county."

"It's one thing to have him on your radar," Pat said. "It's another thing to let catching him become an obsession."

"That's not what's happening here. You need to quit worrying about my fixations and start focusing on a new plan to catch this dirtbag."

Tom could see the harshness of his tone reflected in her pained expression, but apologizing would only serve to acknowledge how right she was. He was in the grip of an obsession he was powerless to resist.

"Ask yourself," Tom said, steering the conversation back on track, "what's the Kingpin's reason to plant a mole in our department?"

"To have eyes and ears on our investigation of him," Pat said.

"We can use that to our advantage. We'll let the Kingpin believe we've dropped further pursuit since his bookie skipped out. I told everyone in the division that I was backing off before I took vacation time. I'll let the men keep thinking that."

"You mean, we'll let everyone think you've put him on a back burner—"

"Until we come up with a plan to point the finger at whoever is leaking information."

"What do you have in mind, boss?"

"What have I trained you to do when you don't know what your next move should be?"

"Go to the experts," Pat said.

"Exactly. I'll be talking with one tonight."

Chapter Eight

Paul arrived home to help Lea prepare an early dinner. His father-in-law was spending the night with them on his way to a policemen's convention where he was scheduled as a guest speaker.

Warren Conley had suffered a stroke shortly before his retirement from a distinguished career with the San Diego Police Department. The partial paralysis which resulted prevented him from pursuing his dream of sailing a boat to South America, but he had re-channeled his energies into writing a book about his exploits as a policeman and lecturing at police academies and conventions.

"I see your father's here already," Paul said, entering the kitchen.

"He's upstairs playing chess with Jon."

"I'll get the grill started. You know Tom has to leave early; he's got late patrol tonight."

"We can eat as soon as he gets here. The meat's marinating, and the veggies are cleaned and ready to grill. As soon as I finish frosting this cake, I'll toss a salad."

"You always have everything under control," Paul said, dipping his finger in a bowl of cream cheese frosting. "I'm glad you made Tom's favorite dessert. I want him in a good mood when I ask him if he considers Jim Mitchell a suspect."

Lea glanced toward the front door. "Here he comes. Get a move on with the grill."

Tom walked through the front door without knocking, sliding his lanky frame onto a bar stool at the kitchen counter. "I saw Warren's car. Is Maddy coming?"

The front door flew open as Maddy entered, carrying a hot dish.

"Scalloped potatoes," she told Tom, placing the casserole on the counter. "Just the way you like them."

"Hey, you two," she greeted Lea and Paul. She sat on a stool next to Tom. "What's up? I haven't heard from you all week."

"I've been busy sorting out the murder at the rodeo. Some of us spend our time getting into messes," he said, tweaking her nose, "the rest of us spend our time sorting messes out."

"Making any progress on possible suspects?" Paul asked.

"Yeah," Maddy said, "as in removing someone from your list?"

"To answer Paul's question first; yes, things are moving along," Tom said. He turned to Maddy. "As for you, sweet thing, I haven't scratched the cowboy off my list, if that's what you're asking."

"Who have you added?" Paul asked, holding his breath as he handed Tom a frosted mug of beer.

"You look a little anxious, buddy. Afraid your client is on my list?" Tom asked. "Is that why you didn't stop by my office like I asked?"

"I got tied up, that's all," Paul said, reaching for another mug.

"If I had guys like you in my interrogation room, my job would be a breeze. You're terrible at telling a lie. So you want to explain why you've been avoiding me?"

"Because I thought you'd jump to the rash conclusion that Jim Mitchell should be one of the names on your list of suspects," Paul responded, testily.

"Let me guess," Tom said, sipping foam dripping down the side of the mug. "You're going to tell me why he shouldn't be."

"That's exactly what I'm—"

"The only way I drop someone from my list is if they have an airtight alibi or no motive."

"That's what I'm trying to tell you," Paul argued. "Jim Mitchell had no motive."

"Save your breath. While you were busy avoiding me, I was gathering information of my own. I found out what was causing hard feelings among the ranchers; a proposed development to be built on three pieces of land: the Benson spread, Cliff Hudson's property, and part of the Miller ranch. The property owners disagreed about selling."

"Here we go again," Maddy objected, hearing the Miller name.

"Don't get riled up," Tom said. "The parcel on the Miller ranch is too small to warrant anyone getting killed over, but it's a key piece of the overall development. The river flows over that strip of land. Whoever owns that parcel has access to water which would make the builder's job a whole lot easier."

"From that aspect, purchase of Miller's piece isn't key to the project. A water right can be granted authorizing water to be diverted from a specified source and put to beneficial, non-wasteful use. A builder could get a permit to divert the water from the Miller property during the development period."

"Good point," Maddy said, punching Tom's arm. "Sounds to me like Paul's blown holes in your theory of accusing Scott."

"Believe me or not, Maddy," Tom said, "but I'm not biased toward building a case against Scott."

"I'm glad to hear that," Maddy pouted.

"In fact," the detective said, turning to Paul with a menacing tone, "I'm more than happy to shift the focus of my investigation. Your client stands to make a seven-figure profit on that housing development. Is that reason enough to knock off the person standing in the way of getting the land he needs? It sure floats my boat for a motive."

"You've got it all wrong," Paul argued.

"As for an airtight alibi, I'll find out about that when I pull your client in for questioning."

"Hold your horses," Lea cautioned. "You may be looking at the wrong person."

"I guarantee he's looking at the wrong person," Maddy said.

"I'm not talking about your friend, Sis." Lea turned to look directly at Tom. "I'm talking about Jim Mitchell. I met with Mitchell's associate, Mike Young, this afternoon."

"Why in sam hill would you do that?" Tom asked, throwing an angry glare in Paul's direction. "Did you give your wife some half-baked reason to butt into this case?"

"I was trying to save you from falsely accusing an innocent person," Paul said.

"You were trying to save your client," Tom said with disgust. "You can tell Jim Mitchell it's not a real estate consultant he needs to retain; it's an attorney."

"Why would my client need an attorney?" Paul asked. "An innocent person has no need for a lawyer."

"Stop, you two," Maddy said. "You sound like two boys squabbling over who's right. Shut up and listen to what Lea has to say."

"Thanks, Sis." Lea handed Maddy a glass of wine, giving the men a moment to cool down. "Mike Young gets profit-sharing from Jim Mitchell's projects. He'll really clean up if the ranchette project goes through."

"What are you suggesting?" Tom asked.

"I'm suggesting that when two of Mike Young's three offers were rejected, Mike pursued the ranchers without Jim's knowledge. The vibes I get from the young man suggest a willingness to cross the line to get deals done. I don't think intimidation would be beyond the realm of tactics he'd use. He may have been behind Albert Benson's crops and livestock being poisoned, and the stream on the Miller ranch being blocked."

"I appreciate your trying to help," Maddy said, "but that sounds like a bit of a stretch."

"You and I have found out what strange things greed leads people to do," Lea insisted.

"She's right," Maddy said, looking at Tom. "Besides, not listening to her has cost you before."

"So far, I don't know if your sleuthing is clearing the air or muddying the water," Tom complained to Lea. "Are you asking me to lay off Jim Mitchell?"

"I'm asking if his associate, Mike Young, could have gone too far in his intimidation tactics with Albert Benson—"

"And ended up killing him," Tom finished.

Paul leaned over and whispered in his wife's ear. "Good job, babe."

* * *

"I thought I heard familiar voices," Warren said, coming down the stairs. "How are you, Tom? Good to see you."

Tom and Maddy stood up, and Tom shook hands with the retired policeman.

"And there's my other beautiful daughter," Warren said, giving Maddy a hug. "Glad you could make it. I missed you last time I was here. You were rehearsing to be in a play, on your way to becoming the next star in the theatrical world."

Maddy grinned. "I turned out to be the fastest shooting star in history."

"The murder that shut down the production was hardly your doing," her father said.

"No, but it was the undoing of my venture into acting," Maddy said.

"The foul act couldn't have happened at a worse time," Paul agreed. "Maddy had only delivered three of her five lines. The audience was waiting breathlessly to hear her other two lines."

"There will be other productions," Warren said, ignoring Paul's sarcasm. "Your mother and I would love to come up and see you in one."

"Sorry, Pop. The whole scene left a bad taste in my mouth. I'm afraid my acting career is over, all three days of it."

"It's okay by me," Tom said, looking at Maddy. "Less chance of you running off to Hollywood leaving me with a broken heart."

"My chances of going to Hollywood are as slim as my chances of breaking your heart," Maddy said. She raised her face to look into his eyes.

"If you think you're not capable of breaking my heart …" Tom said, lifting her chin with his finger.

"Enough," Maddy said, color flooding her cheeks. She picked up her glass and walked into the kitchen. "Pour me another glass of wine, Sis. I'll help with the salad."

"Let's go out to the patio, guys," Paul said. "This conversation is going to turn into women talk. I've got to get the grill going."

* * *

Warren and Tom sat at a glass-topped wicker table sipping beer while Paul tended the grill.

"I'm glad for a chance to talk to you," Tom said. "I've got a situation at the precinct I'd like to run by you. Do you mind talking shop for a minute?"

"You know cops are always willing to swap war stories," Warren said. "What can I help you with?"

Wrinkles creased Tom's brow, and his jaw tightened. His response was blunt.

"I've got a mole in my division."

"That's rough, the worst possible scenario for a senior officer," Warren said. His smile faded as he leaned back. His voice grew husky, close to a whisper. "I've been there. I know how gut-wrenching it can be."

"Yeah, it's hard. Right now, only me and a rookie know that one of my guys is selling out our moves to the worst possible source."

"Let me guess," Warren said, "the Kingpin."

"You got it." Tom shook his head and his shoulders drooped.

"When did you find out?"

"During our under-cover operation at the Card Club. We were trying to bust the scumbag running the Kingpin's illegal gambling operation. The rookie recorded a conversation where the club owner talked about a mole at police headquarters."

"He obviously didn't identify the mole," Warren said, "or you would have busted his chops by now."

"Working with the guys in my squad every day wondering which one is ratting me out is driving me crazy."

"Hard as it is, you've got to stay detached," Warren advised. "Otherwise, you'll start questioning your judgment about the men. You'll start wondering how well you know them. Worse, you'll start questioning if they can be trusted, or whether they've got your back. You can't run operations with those doubts plaguing you. The longer it goes on, the more dangerous it becomes for you and your crew."

"I know," Tom said. He clenched his right hand into a fist and punched it against his palm. "I've got to unravel the mole's identity, and I've got to do it in a hurry. What do you suggest?"

"How many in your division are involved?"

"It's obviously not the rookie, which leaves my other two homicide detectives and two who rotate in from narcotics when I need them."

"The only advice I can give you is based on a similar situation I went through. I reviewed my officers' backgrounds, tracked daily reports, and noted irregular movements or changes in living conditions. I was getting nowhere fast. The uncertainty was destroying me."

"What did you do?"

"I set a trap."

"To flush the traitor out?"

"Exactly. I gave out bogus information regarding the arrival of a valuable cargo shipment to each of the potential moles, telling them they would be assigned to the safe transport of the cargo. The location of the cargo varied for each officer.

"Surveillance cameras were set up at all of the addresses. When armed gunmen showed up to pull off the heist at one of the locations I'd disseminated, we had our mole."

"Was it the one you suspected?"

"No, it wasn't," Warren said. "It taught me a valuable lesson."

"What's that?" Tom asked.

"As policemen, we pride ourselves on understanding human nature; it's essential to our success. But understanding human nature and truly knowing another person are two different things."

"I learned that the hard way," Tom said, flashing a brief smile, "the day I went home, and my wife told me she no longer wanted to be married to a cop."

* * *

"Great grub, honey, as always," Warren told Lea, pushing his chair back from the table and patting his stomach.

"Thanks, Dad, but this was nothing special. Too bad you won't be here Saturday; you could sample dishes from the best chefs in the city."

"Are you talking about the 'Wine and Dine at the Pier' event?" Maddy asked. "I've heard my customers talking about it."

"Lea prepared all the promotional material for it this year," Paul said, patting his wife's hand. "Some of the best brochures she's ever produced."

"They better be," Lea said. "The charities hit up all the big-wigs in the county for this event. It's the biggest fundraiser of the year."

"Your mother will be sorry to miss it. She's always watching gourmet cooking shows on TV. I've never figured out why, she never practices it at home."

"I've still got a couple of complimentary tickets. You want to go, Mad?"

"I'd love to, but I don't have an escort." She propped her chin on her hand, and stared at Tom.

"Don't go batting your eyes at me," Tom said. "You know I hate those stuffy dress-up affairs. Wearing a shirt with a starchy collar and a tie? Thanks, but no thanks. I'll take a plate of ribs like the ones we had tonight any time over those puffy fish pastries which never fill you up."

"After dinner drinks?" Lea asked, carrying empty plates to the kitchen.

"Not for me," Warren said. "I've got to finish the chess game with my grandson. I need all my wits about me."

"How about you, Maddy?" Lea asked. "Irish coffee?"

"You bet. I'm working closing shift tomorrow, I don't need to get up early."

"Tom?"

"Black coffee, please. I've got the late patrol."

"I'll help Lea with the dishes," Paul said. "You two relax."

* * *

Tom and Maddy moved to the patio where they could enjoy the breeze blowing in from the ocean. They sat quietly for several moments gazing at the stars.

Tom raised his coffee mug. "May your joys be as deep as the ocean, and your misfortunes as light as its foam."

"That's lovely, Tom," Maddy said, licking whipped cream from the top of her drink.

"One of the guys at the precinct got married on the beach. It was a toast someone made at his wedding."

"The beach is a beautiful place to get married. Eric and I got married at a ski resort during the biggest snowstorm of the year. Our friends couldn't get to the wedding; the airports were closed. The lodge where we stayed was stranded in six feet of snow. Snowploughs had to dig us out."

"Sounds romantic, considering you're a warm weather girl," Tom said. He could barely conceal a thin-lipped grin. "How did you let him convince you to spend your honeymoon in sub-zero temperatures?"

"Same way I let him talk me into getting married in the first place, but we had our moments. Even though I spent most of the time wrapped in blankets or three layers of sweaters, we managed to build some fires big enough so we could climb out of our clothes at night."

"Yeah, okay. I get the picture," Tom said. He looked away to avoid her gaze.

"Tom Elliot, are you blushing?" Maddy asked, She clapped her hands as color rushed to her own cheeks.

"I just can't picture you as a snow bunny; that's all," he said gruffly.

"I'll admit," she said, "it's not something anyone could talk me into doing now. Thankfully, we learn from our mistakes."

Tom looked down and ran his finger over the rim of the mug. "Do you think marriage was a mistake?"

"Marrying the man I married was a mistake," Maddy said. She pinched her lips between her fingers.

"Will you ever do it again?"

"Marry my ex?" she teased.

"Forget I asked," Tom snapped. "You're making fun of me. This conversation is a joke to you. I suppose marriage is a joke to you, too."

Maddy looked at Tom, surprised at the change in his mood. "No commitment is a joke to me."

"Let's talk about something else," Tom said. He stood up and stretched.

"I'm glad you no longer consider Scott a suspect in Albert Benson's murder," Maddy said, willing to change the subject.

"Did I say that?"

"I thought you told Paul—"

"All I said to Paul was that I might move my focus to his client," Tom said. "You forget it was Scott's gun which was used to kill Benson."

"That pistol could have belonged to any of the competitors in the shooting contest."

"Sorry, your reasoning won't work. The pistol we found at the crime scene had signature markings: five notches cut in the handle, which matches the five trophies I saw displayed at the Miller lodge. Scott's the only local cowboy who's won that many championships."

"All right, I suppose the gun is a reason to suspect him. Do you have anything else on him?"

"I'm no horticulturist, but I could see there was something wrong with the crops at the Benson farm when I was there to interview the son. I picked some samples and sent them to the lab. I should get the results in a day or two."

"What does that have to do with Scott? He'd never poison another man's crops. He has too much respect for ranching to do something like that."

"The way I see it, who better to know exactly how it could be done? And answer me this: why were none of the crops or livestock on the Miller ranch affected?"

"Do you have actual proof or are you making wild accusations out of spite?"

"What are you implying? I have no ill-will toward your cowboy."

"The fact you refer to him as my cowboy says differently. What I'm suggesting is that you're unjustly accusing him because you're jealous of my friendship with him."

"I'm just looking out for you. As far as I'm concerned, you've been put in harm's way on more than one occasion by associating with him."

"Let's get something straight. You can't blame Scott for the hairy situations he and I were in. I got myself in those pickles. Besides, keeping him away from me won't stop me from taking risks. It's not my way to live my life on the sidelines."

"Don't get riled. I know it's in your genes to take risks, and I don't fault you that. In fact, I admire it. But at least your sister knows where to draw lines."

"Lea's got a husband and a kid. She's responsible for more than just herself. She's got reason to listen to Paul when he gets on her case like you're getting on mine."

"Are you telling me that with another person sharing your life you'd be willing to follow orders and stay out of trouble?"

"I don't take orders, you know that," Maddy said. "I barely even take suggestions."

A grin flickered across Tom's face. "I just don't want to see you get hurt again. Besides, I can't help it; the cowboy's arrogance gets my goat."

"Look who's calling someone arrogant. You're cocky yourself sometimes, to the point of being insufferable."

"Are you saying it's a case of 'it takes one to know one'?"

"I'm saying that if you think Scott is arrogant, you don't know him," Maddy said. "Scott's comfortable in his own skin. He doesn't give a hoot about other people's opinion of him. It may come off to you as cockiness, but he doesn't need other people to figure out who he is."

"Since when have you become an expert on human psychology?"

"It's part of what I've gained since moving to Buena Viaje. I'm sorting myself out. I feel more in tune with who I'm meant to be, and I don't define myself by who I'm with anymore. I'm letting myself be me instead of some version of who people think I should be.

"That's what Scott is. He's the only version there is of Scott. He's asked himself the questions 'who am I?' and 'what am I here for?' He's one of the lucky people who's found the answers."

"Do you ever ask yourself those questions?" Tom asked.

"Oh, sure, there are days when I wonder when my life will add up, if ever."

"You're no different than the rest of us," Tom said. "We all want to be significant. We want our life to stand for something."

"You seem to be doing what you're meant to be doing," Maddy told him. "What does it feel like?"

"It feels like not worrying if something is the right thing to do or how to do it. The know-how comes when you need it."

"Do you ever question if chasing bad guys is the right thing for you to do?"

"It's one of the few things I know for sure, that putting criminals behind bars is what I'm meant to do."

"You sound pretty sure of yourself, Detective," Maddy teased, "In fact, you sound downright arrogant."

"That's what I love about you," Tom said. He smiled at the way she'd turned the cards on him. "You question the way I see things and make me look at things differently."

"You do need your point of view tweaked once in a while," Maddy said.

"Hold your thought," Tom said, answering his cell phone. "It's the coroner."

When he finished, he stood up abruptly. "I have to leave."

"Where are you going? Did I say something wrong?"

"Not at all, but I need to take care of something I should be looking at differently."

Chapter Nine

Tom and Pat were almost at the end of their late shift when they were summoned to a motel in the low rent district of Buena Viaje. The motel was a run-down building the vice squad had visited on frequent occasions.

Tom checked in with the clerk at the front desk, a scrawny, unshaven man who hid the magazine he was leafing through when the police entered. "What is it this time, your customers breaking up furniture again?"

"Good evening to you, too, Lieutenant," the man said, jerking his head toward the garbage bins at the back of the motel. "Someone reported seeing a body back there. I've been too busy to check it out."

"Yeah, I can see how busy you are," Tom sneered, returning to the car. "Let's go, Fisher. We might have a stiff on our hands."

From the space where Tom parked, the outline of a woman's body was barely visible. Pat walked over and kneeled beside her, feeling for a pulse. "She's breathing, but barely. From the heavy makeup, tight skirt, and stilettos, I'd say she's a working girl. We need an ambulance; she's been badly beaten."

"Call it in and stay with her while I knock on some doors. She probably got dumped by someone in one of these rooms. My guess is nobody staying at this joint is going to answer our questions. I'll be lucky to get them to answer the door."

Fisher stayed with the body until the paramedics arrived before catching up with her boss.

"Did you get anything out of her?" Tom asked.

"She was rambling about needing her daddy and something about it being her fault."

"Bottom dollar the daddy in this case is her pimp." Tom shook his head. "This kind of thing disgusts me. Most of these girls are run-aways from home living at the mercy of these scumbags. One wrong move and they end up like her. Or they're used up, maybe ruined by drugs, by the time they're thirty years old and thrown back on the streets where they were found after the douche bags make a fortune on them."

"You sound bitter," Pat said.

"There was a girl who lived down the street from me growing up. We weren't close, but we always talked when we rode the bus to school. On days when I wasn't playing sports, we'd walk home from school together.

"In high school, she started running with a bad crowd. She was having problems at home. Her dad was a drunk, the nasty kind, and her older brother got busted for drugs. My friends and I turned our backs on her.

"She ran away our senior year; never graduated. I didn't see her again until several years later.

"I was on one of my first patrols fresh out of the Academy. We responded to a call at a local hotel. It was my first dead body. The room indicated a call-girl setup.

"I still remember her lifeless eyes. They appeared to be nothing more than icy, colored marbles. I hardly recognized her. She and I were the same age, but she looked years older.

"The other officer made some lewd comments, and I took a swing at him. He didn't report me; he said he was doing me a favor because it was a rookie reaction. I didn't let on that I knew her.

"She had fake identification, so no one would have known who she was. Except me; I knew. On my day off, I drove to my neighbor's house to tell her mother. I was sure her father wouldn't care."

Pat felt his pain. "Is that one of the reasons why bringing down the Kingpin is so important to you?"

"I was never able to prove she was part of his operation, but he preys on runaway girls. Putting him behind bars would keep him from ruining other girls' lives."

He rubbed his hand across his forehead like someone trying to dispel a bad memory. "It's a sour note to end the day on. Go home, Pat. I'll go to the hospital and fill them in on the details."

* * *

Tom was beat by the time he arrived at the hospital to confer with the nurse in charge of the night shift. He gladly accepted the coffee she offered.

"What do we have here, Lieutenant?"

"Most likely a prostitute who made her pimp unhappy. If clients play this rough, they get scared and leave the body in the room. We found her by the garbage. It could have been a message from her sugar-daddy."

"We're receiving more of these victims lately," the nurse said. Tom detected sympathy in the woman's voice. "The game seems to be getting more brutal."

"We're seeing the same increase in sex-trafficking that you are. The internet has changed the game by taking these girls off the streets and hiding them behind closed doors. The girls are typically sold on a website, locked in hotel rooms, and forced to have sex for money, sometimes up to fifteen times a day before handing all the cash over to a pimp."

"This girl hardly looks the type from what I could see under the bruises and cut lip," the nurse said.

"There are no types. Any girl who is disconnected from her family can fit the profile. The game cuts across all race, gender, and socio-economic factors." He threw his paper cup in the trash. "What's her condition, can I talk to her?"

"Most of her wounds are superficial. She's got a cracked rib which will have to heal on its own," the nurse said, noting the patient's chart. "She's awake, but not for long. We've given her a sedative."

"I'll only be a few minutes," Tom said.

"Do you think she'll tell you who did this to her?"

"Probably not, but I've got to try. Most of these women have been convinced by their traffickers and through experience that no adults or police officers can be trusted to help them. They come across as belligerent or refuse to talk.

"They're afraid of their handlers and don't believe anyone can get them out of the situation they're in. The mental manipulation and control these traffickers have over women is the most challenging aspect for us and the welfare agencies who try to help them."

"From what I've seen of her, she'll have more than a beating to recover from," the nurse said. "There are track marks on her arm."

"The man I suspect of running this prostitution ring also heads up a narcotics operation. He uses his easy access to drugs to keep girls under control. Drugs and alcohol help the victimized girls numb themselves so they can cope with what they're being forced to do. A drug or alcohol abuse program is usually needed to help victims get out and stay out of the business."

"But you're still willing to try?"

"When you see a young person rescued from sex-trafficking, it's one of the most inspiring things in the world."

* * *

The young woman's eyes were closed with her head resting on a pillow when Tom entered the room. He could visualize her heavily made-up as most women in the trade appeared when he arrested them. With her face scrubbed clean and bandaged, she looked innocent and vulnerable. He hated to disturb her peace.

"Excuse me, Miss." He looked at the driver's license the nurse had given him. "Amber, are you awake?"

Her head turned and her eyes opened, but she didn't sit up.

"I'm Detective Elliot. My partner and I found you tonight at the motel. How are you feeling?"

"How do I look like I'm feeling?"

Tom knew from her sarcastic tone where the interview was headed. "I need to get some information about what happened to you."

"I slipped down the stairs and fell against the dumpster." Even makeup wouldn't hide the ugly twisted expression which spread across her face.

"Maybe you were pushed."

"Like I said, I'm clumsy. I don't walk so good in three-inch heels."

"What were you doing at the motel? Your name wasn't on the register for that room."

"I was visiting a friend, a school buddy from my old neighborhood. Long time, no see; we were having a reunion."

Tom felt like he'd been kicked in the gut, or maybe it was bad karma.

"I wish I could verify your story, but whoever signed for the room has disappeared. Guess he wasn't a good enough buddy to hang around to help you after you fell down the stairs."

"He left before me. He couldn't have seen it happen."

"I'm sure you wouldn't mind giving me his name. An address would help, too," Tom said. He pulled out a notepad.

"My accident had nothing to do with him," she said.

"Look, Amber, I'm only trying to help. If you're a victim, I'd like to find whoever did this to you."

"How many times do I have to tell you this is my own stupid fault?"

"You know what? I feel sorry for you because you might truly feel being beaten is your fault. But let me give you my version of what happened. I think your pimp came to collect his money after your john left. Your daddy, as you called him at the scene, got mad and pushed you down the stairs.

"What did you do to set him off? Did you hold back some of your night's take, or maybe you were disrespecting him, and he was trying to teach you some manners."

"My personal life is none of your business." The injured woman's eyes glazed over to match the blank expression on her face.

"I don't doubt you have reason to be afraid of him," he said, "but we can protect you. Give us his name, and we'll make sure he never hurts you again."

"How easy you make things sound," she said. She was beginning to slur her words. "Go back to your world, copper. Let me drift off to never-never land for a few hours before I have to return to mine."

Tom alerted the nurse on his way out, handing her his card. "Let me know if she has any visitors, or if anyone comes to pay her bill."

Chapter Ten

The next morning at breakfast, Paul seemed preoccupied.

"Something on your mind?" Lea asked.

"I think I'll drop by to see Jim Mitchell on my way into the office. If I know Tom, he'll take that tip you gave him last night and run with it by going to speak directly with Mike Young. I'll feel better if I give Jim a heads-up, so he won't think I've gone behind his back with suspicions about his associate."

"He can't help but think that; it's exactly what we did."

"I sent you in order to prevent unwarranted accusations," Paul said. "That's the part Jim won't know unless I tell him. I'm sure he'll understand we were acting in his best interests."

"Jim may understand that, but I'm not sure Mike will see it that way."

"All the more reason to get ahead of it now that Tom's involved."

"Good luck. Let me know how it goes."

* * *

Lea answered her phone later. "Hi, Tom. If you're looking for Paul, he's left the house already."

"That's all right, it's you I'm looking for."

Lea's interest was piqued. "What can I do for you?" she asked and set aside the file on her desk.

"Are you still a volunteer at the Second Chance Children's Center?"

"Yes, I am. I hope one of the kids isn't in trouble with you."

"Not a kid living there now," Tom said, "but I've got a victim in the hospital I think you may know. When I checked for prior arrests, I found juvenile charges for shop-lifting. The name of her court-appointed special advocate was noted in her court appearances."

"I've been an advocate for several young people in the past, but they've all aged out of the program. Those kids turn eighteen years of age and the bottom drops out for them. No more public funds are available, and private donations subsidize them for less than a year."

"Do you stay in touch with them?"

"I try to," she said. "It's up to them once they're officially released from the program. In the best case scenario, the young person can return home to a safe family environment where the parents or siblings have received counseling. In the worst case, their eighteenth birthday signifies freedom to them. They want nothing more to do with authority figures, and shut off further contact. I've had both kinds of experience with the kids I advocated for. Who are you referring to?"

"Amber Owens."

Lea gasped, but didn't respond.

"Lea, did you hear me?"

"I heard you, but I wish I hadn't." She took a deep breath. "I'm sorry to hear Amber's in trouble, although I can't say I'm surprised. She had no family to return to when her stay at Second Chance was over. Her mother's a heroin addict. I always suspected her father of being abusive, but she never accused him."

"She sounds like easy prey for some pimp to give her the family she didn't have," Tom said. "These girls get lured into the game by the illusion of love and a secure future. What makes them stay is the fear of being beaten, outed as whores, or left for dead. That might have been the outcome for Amber if we hadn't found her in time."

"Has she told you what happened?" Lea asked. "Who did this to her?"

"I've run into a closed door. She's like other victims of sex-trafficking. When they come in contact with law enforcement, they aren't exactly running into our arms begging for help. They're scared, and they don't trust police. Maybe they're threatened by their trafficker, maybe not. Either way, they're not usually cooperative in identifying themselves as victims."

"What do you want me to do? I'll do anything to help Amber."

"I'm hoping she might open up to you," Tom said. "You'll have difficulty getting her to talk unless you can break through the protective barrier she's thrown up, but she knows you advocated for her before. She may still believe you're on her side. At least, you can use a softer approach."

"You mean, instead of slamming her in an interview room with bars on the windows and metal chairs, I can meet her in a room with sofas and pillows and offer her a hamburger and soda."

"That's the idea," Tom agreed. "I know Second Chance provides housing and counseling for women rescued from trafficking situations. If you can convince her she has alternatives other than returning to her pimp, whether it's getting a job, going to school, or moving away to get a fresh start, she might be more willing to help us.

"You won't have much time. The hospital is releasing her today or tomorrow, and I don't have charges to hold her. Unless her pimp's thrown her out for good, he'll be there to pay the bill and take her. He may be through using her as a whore, but he'll want to make sure she doesn't tell us anything. He may even feel he needs to shut her up permanently."

"I'll do what I can, but I can't make any promises."

"She may be a lost cause."

"The only lost cause," Lea said, motivated by his comment, "is one we give up on before we enter the struggle."

* * *

Lea went to the hospital during early visiting hours and was directed to Amber's room. The patient was propped up on pillows staring at a television screen. Lea was glad to see the other bed of the shared room was empty.

The young woman had changed since Lea last saw her but not in a good way. Her complexion was dull, and her once luxurious hair was dry and brittle. The eyes above the black-and-blue bruises had a hollowed-out look.

"Hello, Amber," Lea said, sitting in a chair beside the bed.

"What are you doing here?" Amber asked, pulling the sheet to her chin.

"Detective Elliot called and asked me to visit you."

"He had no right, I didn't ask for you." She squeezed her face like a pouting child.

"We're worried about you," Lea said. She spoke in a calm, soothing voice. "Why didn't you ever call? I had hoped we'd stay in touch after you left Second Chance."

"Yeah, well, I was busy trying to survive. As soon as my monthly allowance from the state expired, I had to support myself."

"Your family couldn't help?" Lea asked, but she was reluctant to open wounds.

"I can't believe you're even asking me that question. Did you honestly expect my all-American family would be waiting with open arms to welcome me home?"

"I arranged for you to attend night school to get your GED. How did you like it?"

"I dropped out after two classes." Amber lowered her head like a child anticipating a scolding. "I had to change my address and phone number to get the counselor at Second Chance to stop bugging me."

"I'm not here to criticize or to judge you," Lea said. She reached over, placing her hand on top of Amber's. The young woman didn't pull her hand away. "But I would like to know why we're having this conversation in a hospital room."

Amber reached for a tissue from the box beside her bed, and dabbed at her eyes and nose. "I'm sorry, Lea. You've always tried to be a friend. I shouldn't take my problems out on you."

"That's what I'm here for. I may not be able to help, but I'm willing to listen. Maybe together, we can sort things out."

Amber leaned her head back and closed her eyes. "Just so you know, I did make an effort to patch things up at home."

"What happened?"

"That was a wasted effort if there ever was one," the girl said, looking miserable. "My mom was so whacked, she barely knew who I was from one day to the next. I wasn't about to hang around and give my dad a chance to use me as a punching bag.

"I ran into a friend from school, a fellow drop-out. She invited me to her place. She had a nice apartment, spending money, and a cool wardrobe. I asked how she paid for it. She told me about some guy who was taking care of her, and offered to introduce me. She said if he liked me, he might help me out."

Lea didn't comment, unwilling to interrupt her story.

"Joey was real nice when I met him." Amber picked at the corner of the bed-sheet, and her lips turned upward in a half-smile. "We started going out. He took me to parties where there were free drinks and drugs, and everyone drove flashy cars. He bought me gifts, and we talked about our future. Once he'd shown me the life we could have, he hinted at how much money I could make dating other men."

"Couldn't you see how wrong it was, what he was suggesting?" Lea asked. Her heart was breaking over what she was hearing.

"Joey showed me a picture of the house we would buy and live in together," Amber said, her voice trembling. "He said I'd just have to do it for a little while, and then we'd never have to worry about money again.

"I thought it was the sacrifice I had to make to get the dream life we talked about. He said we'd get married and have kids, and I could give them all the things my parents never gave me."

"And you believed him?" Lea tried to hide her skepticism so Amber wouldn't feel ashamed.

"He told me all the things I wanted to hear; it was like he was reading my mind. I didn't realize how badly I wanted those things until he made me believe I could have them."

"When did you realize Joey's stories were lies?"

"The first time I said I didn't want to turn tricks anymore. I told him we had enough money to start our life together. I begged him, but he laughed at me." A tremor ran through her body. "And then he beat me."

"Why didn't you run away when you realized how dangerous he was?"

"I knew I should leave, but I was trapped," Amber said. She twisted the bed-sheet between her fingers. "Joey got inside my head. I felt like he had hold of me from the inside, like he was controlling my mind."

"What about your friend, couldn't she help?"

"I found out she isn't a friend," Amber said. Her voice turned angry and bitter. "She's his recruiter. She draws girls in for him, like a spider spinning a web. Joey has a whole stable of women working for him."

An oppressive silence hung in the air. Amber's pale complexion reflected the toll that telling her story had taken. Lea felt drained herself.

"What happened last night, before the police found you?"

"My last date had left the motel room. Joey came to pick up the night's take. I talked to him again about leaving the business. I told him I'd pay him a lot of money if he'd let me go and leave me alone."

"How did he respond?"

"He spit in my face. Asked me where I'd get money for an exit fee since I turned over all my money to him."

"What did you tell him?"

"I didn't have a chance before the maniac totally lost it. He accused me of holding out, asking how much money I'd stashed away.

"I told him I turned over every penny I earned, but he didn't believe me. The last thing I remember was blood spurting out my nose as his fist hit my face. I must have blacked out. When I came to, I was in this hospital room. The cop who sent you came to see me, but I don't remember much of the conversation."

"I'm sure you remember him asking you to tell him who did this, so he can protect you."

A high-pitched laugh from Amber sent a shiver through Lea.

"Your cop friend can't protect me. Once you're part of the organization, you never get out unless they have no more use for you. Then they throw you out like a wounded animal.

"Joey will give me time to miss him. When he thinks I've learned my lesson, he'll come to find me and suck me back into the business."

"You've got to get away, Amber. Your life could be in danger if he thinks you'd turn him in."

Amber shook her head. "Joey knows no one would be that stupid. He has nothing to worry about."

"Tom can protect you. We'll help you start a new life."

"I know what you're after. You want me to rat Joey out in return for witness protection, but what you don't understand is that I don't want to go away." Her tone was belligerent, but her eyes searched for answers. "You may think I don't have anything to lose because I don't have much of a home here, but this is where I've grown up. This town is all I know, it's all I want to know."

"I'm not saying you have to move away to start over, but you need help to turn your life around. There's no place you can run to which will be any different unless you straighten out who you are. You'll have the same things to face anywhere else that you're facing here.

"The first step is to let Tom help you break away from this man who's destroying you. You can't start a new life until you end the one you're living."

"Are you crazy! You don't know what you're saying. Helping the cops is a sure way to end my life, not to start a new one."

"No, it's not," Lea said. "I know you're afraid of Joey, but don't you see? He's brainwashed you into feeling threatened by him, that's how he controls you. He knows you have no family support system, and he's separated you from any other source of help. He wants you to believe he's the only person in your life and that you have no one else to turn to.

"He's convinced you that you can't survive without him, and that you're not worthy of having a better life. He's stripped you of your belief in yourself."

An instant passed with Lea not knowing if Amber's response was one of anger or regret. The young woman's body rocked back and forth, and her hospital gown slipped off her shoulder.

"Look me in the eyes and tell me," Lea said, lifting Amber's chin and watching tears stream down her face, "that the way he's made you feel is how a man who loves a woman wants her to feel."

"It's not that I don't want my life to be different," Amber sobbed, "but I don't have the strength to change it."

"You may not have the strength to do it by yourself because Joey's made you feel that way, but you're not alone anymore. There are other people in your corner now."

* * *

They spent the next half-hour making plans for Amber's future. Before leaving, Lea remembered to ask Tom's question. "One more thing. Joey isn't running his operation as a lone wolf. Do you know who his boss is?"

"I've never met him, but he's called when I've been with Joey," Amber said. "Those are the only times I've seen Joey nervous, scared even. He's usually an arrogant SOB, but when he gets those calls, he turns into a shriveling 'yes' man. I asked him once why the guy shakes him up. He slapped me and told me to mind my own business. Is it important?"

"Nothing for you to worry about," Lea said, pressing the young woman's hand. "I have to go meet my sister now, but I'll call Lieutenant Elliot to make arrangements for your safety at the hospital and a place for you to stay.

"I'll visit you tomorrow. In the meantime, keep your chin up. The detective will have Joey behind bars in no time. He'll never be able to hurt you again."

* * *

Lea sat in her car in the parking garage and tapped Tom's number on her cell phone.

"Hey, Lea. Hope you've got good news about Amber."

"Yes and no. She's ready to accept help to get out of the business."

"What's her pimp's name?" Tom asked, cutting to the chase.

"The only name she could give me is 'Joey', but she's willing to look at mug shots and identify him in a line-up. She wants immunity from soliciting charges and her record of previous arrests expunged."

"Great. I'll talk to the district attorney; that should be do-able. What about his boss? Can she finger his boss?"

"That's the bad news. Whenever his boss called, Joey made her leave the room. She doesn't know his name, and she didn't hear any of their conversations."

A brief silence registered Tom's disappointment. "Maybe if I talk to her—"

"No way, Tom," Lea warned. "She's worried enough about Joey. If you pressure her about her pimp's boss, it may scare her away. I don't want to lose her. If you ever want my help again, don't pursue that line of questioning. It's a dead-end."

"Okay," Tom said. "I've heard you use that tone enough times with Paul to know that arguing is pointless. I'll do it your way."

"When she's released from the hospital, I'll take her some clothes and other things she might need. In the meantime, I'll contact Second Chance and line up a safe place where she can stay until you've arrested Joey. I don't think she should go back to her apartment in case he shows up looking for her."

"I agree. We'll send someone to guard her room. When the hospital discharges her, the officer will take her to the living quarters you've arranged. After a couple days of rest, we'll bring her to the station to go through mug shots."

"I'll call you as soon as I've found a place for her."

"Thanks, Lea, you've been a big help. I owe you."

"All you owe me is keeping Amber safe. I'll contact people who can help her get her life back on track. The rest will be up to her."

Chapter Eleven

Paul was glad to see only one car parked in front of the construction trailer at the condominium site. Jim Mitchell was seated at his desk when Paul walked in. He looked up in surprise.

"Two unannounced visits in one week. Something else come up at City Hall?"

"Sorry I didn't call before coming," Paul said. "Can you spare a few minutes?"

Jim put aside the papers he was working on and pointed to a chair in front of his desk. "What's on your mind?"

"I hesitated about having this conversation," Paul said taking a seat, "but you're a client and a friend. I'd feel remiss if we didn't discuss what's troubling me."

Jim leaned back. "You've got my attention."

"You told me you aren't pursuing the ranchette project east of town, but there are indications that Mike Young is still trying to buy land and acting in an overly-ambitious manner. He may be crossing lines that shouldn't be crossed."

Jim frowned and leaned forward. "He hasn't discussed any new activity with me. As far as I know, he hasn't had further contact with any of the property owners."

"I know he's met with at least one of the farmers. What's worse, there are signs of under-handed, possibly illegal, dealings."

"What kind of under-handed dealings?"

"I'd rather not be more specific," Paul said.

"I don't know where you're getting your information, but I find the accusation hard to believe." Jim's voice had taken on a defensive quality.

"Has Mike been above-board in all of his previous negotiations?" Paul asked.

Jim remained silent for several moments, doodling on the blotter on his desk. He finally sat back and folded his arms across his chest. He appeared unperturbed. "I appreciate your concern. I know you believe you're looking out for my best interests, but I assure you, you don't need to worry about Mike.

"He's got the typical aggressive sales personality. It may appear overly-zealous to you, but I've found it to be quite useful in negotiations. It's a viable offset to the laid-back approach people expect from me."

"I don't mean to be critical or to overstep my bounds," Paul assured him.

"You forget we were ambitious like that early in our careers," Jim said, "insensitive about stepping on people's toes. Mike will adopt a more diplomatic approach as he ages, just as we did."

"I beg to differ with you," Paul said. "Neither of us has ever had Mike's slant on business. You know that as well as I do."

"I suppose," Jim relented, "but you've coached kids' sports. Who did you prefer to coach; the gung-ho kid you had to rein in, or the less-aggressive kid you had to motivate all the time?"

"I can't argue with that," Paul said.

"Don't worry. I can rein Mike in anytime I need to. Besides, he knows I wouldn't condone anything illegal."

"Your statement implies Mike would be willing to do something illegal if he thought you'd condone it."

The sharpness of Jim's next question signaled dwindling patience. "Do you have anything more specific to discuss?"

Paul's response was blunt. "The police are interested in the potential profit from that development as a motive for Albert Benson's murder."

"Who are they looking at as a suspect, me or my associate?"

"They were looking at you," Paul said. "After Lea's discussion with Mike, they've turned their attention to him."

"So Lea's interest in marketing this condominium project was a ploy to interview Mike as a potential suspect?" Jim asked. There was anger in his voice.

Paul came quickly to her defense. "Lea's only trying to protect you, the same as me. I brought her in when I found out you were under suspicion by the police."

"How did you think she could help?"

"I simply asked her to use her inquisitive nature and instinct to sense if anything was off about Mike. You know how women are with their uncanny intuition. It can be astonishingly accurate, although that's something I seldom admit to Lea."

"I understand," Jim said. He relaxed, and the frown on his face disappeared. "My wife's the same. But are you saying Lea and the police have reason to suspect Mike?"

"The investigation is still underway, but the police are anxious to speak with him. I'm here to alert you before they show up unannounced at your corporate office."

"Should I warn Mike?"

"It would be better to let the chips fall where they may, but I didn't want you to be in the dark about what's going on."

"Thanks for being so candid." Jim pushed his chair away from his desk and stood up. "I understand your hesitation in bringing this to me."

"Let me know if there's anything I can do." Paul reached to shake hands.

"I will," Jim said, extending his hand. "Don't worry; your honesty hasn't damaged our business relationship. I wouldn't expect anything less from you, and I still want to receive a proposal from your intuitive wife."

* * *

Lea received Paul's call relaying his conversation with Jim Mitchell. "I hope Jim took it the right way."

"Jim understood my need to have the conversation. He appreciated my candor."

"How do you feel?"

"Much better," Paul said. "I hope our reservations about Mike prove to be unfounded. Regardless, Jim knows we're both looking out for him. He's still anxious for you to submit a marketing proposal."

"That's good to hear. I need some more information on the company to finish my submission. I'm going to the corporate office—"

"You aren't thinking of meeting with Mike Young again?"

"No, I'll leave him to Tom. I'm getting the information I need from Helen Taylor."

"All right, I'll see you tonight."

* * *

Lea checked in with the receptionist at Mitchell Development Company. "I'm here to pick up some information from Mr. Mitchell's secretary."

"Go on back," the receptionist said. "If Helen's not at her desk, let me know and I'll page her for you."

Walking down the hall to the executive area, Lea could see that neither Jim Mitchell nor Mike Young was in his office. Helen Taylor was nowhere in sight. She jotted a message on a post-it note and stuck it on Helen's chair.

She glanced over her shoulder before walking quickly into Mike's office.

There were no files on his desk and his in-box was empty, but his computer screen was open to a directory. She saw a folder labeled Ranchette Project.

She clicked on the folder. It opened to a document titled 'Land Purchase'.

As her eyes darted across the spreadsheet, she heard the sound of a familiar voice approaching. Racing around the desk, she almost collided with Mike Young.

"Back so soon with a marketing proposal?" he asked.

"I'm picking up some background information on the corporation from Helen."

"What are you doing in my office?"

"Helen said she'd leave a package for me," Lea said. "It wasn't on her desk. I thought she might have left it in your office."

"There's nothing in my office for you." Mike's tone made Lea's heart skip a beat.

"No problem," she said. She turned to make a hasty retreat. "I'll ask the receptionist to locate Helen."

"The timing of your appearance is interesting," Mike said, "so soon after I received a call from a police detective arranging an interview. You wouldn't know anything about that, would you?"

"Nothing at all," Lea replied. She moved toward the door.

"You appear to be putting together more than a bid to do our promotions," he said, extending an arm in front of her, blocking the doorway. "I advise you to stick to creating brochures."

At that moment, Helen Taylor appeared. She glanced quickly between Lea and Mike.

"Good to see you, Lea," she said. "I have the information you requested."

Mike lowered his arm, and Lea brushed past him.

At Helen's desk, Lea accepted the envelope which was offered.

"Did you get any other useful information?" Helen asked.

"Mike commented on my timing, but my timing's not nearly as interesting as the dates of his meetings with the ranchers."

Chapter Twelve

Tom called Pat Fisher's cell phone and left a message for her to meet him at the Pier for lunch.

When she arrived, she found him bending over a plate of food at a table in front of the fish stand. "I thought you were springing for a real meal at the seafood restaurant."

"This is a seafood restaurant. Order a fish taco and quit complaining," he told her, wiping hot sauce from his chin.

When Pat returned to the table carrying a plate of crab cakes, Tom filled her in on Lea's meeting with Amber. "Amber's scared, but she's willing to cooperate."

"Asking Lea to intervene was smart, boss. The vic was never going to agree to work with the police."

"That's why I've got extra bars on my sleeve, Rookie." Tom smiled, always ready to soak in a compliment. "This is the way I see the sting. We won't keep Amber in one of our safe houses. Lea's making arrangements through Second Chance for a place for her to stay. We'll put the word out on the street that we've got a prostitute in custody who's ready to turn over her pimp, but we won't let our informants know where we've got her stashed."

"Amber's pimp will want to get hold of her," Pat reasoned, "so he'll need to find out the location."

"Right. He'll ask the Kingpin to get the address from the mole planted in our division. I'll give each of the squad members a different location where we're holding Amber. I've ordered surveillance cameras set up at each of the sites. Once I've given the officers the false leads, all we need to do is sit back and wait to see which house gets hit."

"What if Joey decides it's too risky to spring Amber from a safe house?"

"Did I say Joey would try to spring Amber?" Tom asked. "I agree he'd consider it too big a chance to take if all he wants to do is put her back on the streets. But if Amber is staying with us instead of going back to him, he'll know she's made a deal. I think he'll want to get rid of her permanently. If he doesn't, the Kingpin will."

"But she told Lea she couldn't identify the Kingpin."

"The Kingpin doesn't know that. From our previous experience with the dead bodies he leaves in his wake, we know he won't tolerate loose ends. If Joey doesn't take care of business, the Kingpin will have no qualms about sending one of his hired guns to make sure she can't implicate him."

"Since she won't be there for anyone to kill, we won't have grounds to charge whoever comes for her with more than breaking-and-entering."

"Best case, we catch whoever goes for the girl and charge them with attempted murder. Worse case, it won't matter because we'll have what we're after. The cameras will show us where Joey or a hit man shows up. We'll know by the location who tipped them off.

"Let's get back to the precinct." He threw his empty paper plate in the recycle bin. "I'm anxious to set our little trap in play."

* * *

Tom called the squad together in the conference room. "We've had a break. Pat and I were called to a motel by the beach last night. The desk clerk called in a body by the dumpster."

"Dead?" The question came from Jack Jones, known around the precinct as JJ.

"It was a prostitute beaten and left for dead."

"Customer service complaint from her john?" JJ joked. Everyone except Tom and Pat laughed.

"Knock it off," Tom ordered. "She's willing to pick out her pimp in a line-up."

"A prostitute co-operating with the police and ratting out a pimp? What did it take to convince her to do that, boss?"

"I wasn't the one who convinced her, I used an intermediary," Tom said. "We'll get the witness settled in a safe house when she's released from the hospital. She'll come in the next day to look at mug shots. As soon as she fingers someone, we can schedule a line-up."

"What's the rush, Lieutenant?" Pat asked, leading the conversation where she knew Tom wanted it to go. "You aren't usually this interested in arresting pimps."

"Because it sounds like her sugar-daddy has been receiving orders from a higher source."

"You mean higher as in Kingpin?" Pat asked.

"Bingo," Tom said, paying attention to the faces of his officers. "With her identification, our case against the pimp should be strong enough to persuade him to turn on his boss in exchange for a reduced sentence. If we're lucky and he's got priors, this may be his third strike which makes him ripe to deal."

All the men seemed eager. Tom wasn't able to pick out signs of any officer being distressed at the news.

Pat picked up the cue on the Lieutenant's glance. "Which safe house is she stashed at?"

"I'll give the information out on an as-needed basis to the officer I assign to guard her."

"I'll volunteer," JJ offered. "I wouldn't mind hanging out with a cute little squeeze all day."

The others snickered before Tom responded. "It's not that kind of surveillance. It will be a boring day sitting in an unmarked car outside to make sure she has no visitors."

He walked toward the door. "That's all for now. We'll convene tomorrow morning for updates.

"JJ, you're riding with Rick today. I've got a meeting with the Superintendent. Take Pat over to the yard to get an unmarked vehicle. She can pick me up after my meeting."

"Roger that, Lieutenant," JJ said, throwing a mock salute in Tom's direction. He turned to Pat and Rick. "C'mon, you two, I'm driving. We're stopping at a drive-through on the way. I haven't had breakfast."

Pat turned up her nose. "Did you ever consider having something healthier for breakfast, JJ?"

"Like pancakes and bacon?"

"Like yogurt or oatmeal."

"You and I don't live on the same planet, Pat." JJ laughed and led the way to the lockers.

* * *

Tom alerted the software tech to intercept all calls in and out from each officer's cell phone for the next forty-eight hours. It was a long shot, but on the off-chance the guilty officer would slip up and use his own phone instead of a burner phone to tip off the Kingpin, he wanted to know about it.

"I want to find out who they're calling and when. Log it all. I'll check with you later to get the results."

Tom went to his office and propped his feet on his desk. He reviewed the plan in his mind. He would make sure the officers didn't communicate with each other by waiting until the end of the shift the next day before assigning each squad member a location to guard Amber. All he could do now was sit back and wait.

Waiting was the worst part of his job. The thought of the Kingpin slipping through his fingers a second time weighed heavily. He needed a distraction.

He wouldn't have long to wait before one would arrive in the form of an emergency call from Maddy.

* * *

The three officers picked up their gear and piled into a squad car.

"You're in the back, Rookie," Rick said, sliding onto the front passenger seat.

Pat couldn't help but notice the contrast between the two officers in front of her. The hair loss on the back of Rick's head, the lines etched on his forehead, and the dark circles under his eyes were signs of a man with small children and responsibilities at home. Besides his youthful looks, JJ moved with the swagger of someone without a care in the world.

"When are you going to stop treating me like a second-class citizen?" she asked.

Pat was in an awkward position. She wanted to be accepted by the members of the homicide squad, but she felt they resented her. And now she was working under-cover with Tom to bust one of them as a mole.

"When your probation period is over," Rick said. "Don't worry. After the way you handled yourself on the Card Club bust, it should be sooner rather than later."

Pat noticed JJ tighten his grip on the steering wheel. "Are you still pissed because Tom picked me to go under-cover on the operation at the Card Club instead of you?"

"You didn't have enough experience," JJ said.

"It turned out pretty well."

"Except Mickey got away. He was our best link to the Kingpin." JJ pulled behind a car stopped at the drive-through window. "That wouldn't have happened if I'd been under-cover on the assignment."

"Are you saying you're a master of going under-cover?"

"I sure as heck know more than a rookie."

"Yeah, well, you need to get over yourself, JJ," Pat said, staring at the menu.

"The Lieutenant's obsessed with bringing down the Kingpin," Rick grumbled.

"Something wrong with that?" Pat asked, tuning into Rick's complaint.

"His obsession can be dangerous to the rest of the squad. If he's not thinking clearly, he's likely to put us in a high-risk situation."

"I haven't seen him do anything yet to jeopardize our safety," JJ said. He leaned toward the speaker and placed their order before turning back to Rick. "Dangerous situations are part of the job. Our ops don't come with safety nets. Besides, it's just his way. Once he latches on, he's like a bulldog; he won't let go."

Rick shrugged. "No criticism intended. I'm just saying—"

"What's the matter, Rick, getting cold feet?" Pat asked. She handed money to JJ when he stopped at the first window.

"Heck, no. Can't a person make an observation around here without getting jumped on?"

"You seem a little jumpy yourself lately," JJ said. He paid the cashier and drove to the pick-up window. "Something else bothering you?"

"Filling in for you last night didn't help things at home," Rick said.

"I told you I'd make it up to you," JJ replied.

"That's the second shift this month I've covered for you."

"Yeah, JJ, what's up with that?" Pat asked. "It's not like you."

"Stomach problems, that's all."

"Maybe you should see a doctor," Pat suggested.

"Forget sending him to a quack," Rick said. He took the drinks JJ passed and handed one back to Pat. "I told lover-boy here to suck it up and quit calling in sick. For all I know, he was on a hot date."

Pat took her drink from Rick. "We aren't all supermen like you. He could have been sick. Give the guy a break."

"Tell it to my wife," Rick said. "She's on my case for the over-time I've put in covering for this slacker."

"She should be happy you're bringing home some extra bread," JJ said. He handed Rick the paper bag and drove away from the window.

"You'd think so, wouldn't you?" Rick said, handing out the food. "With two kids and another on the way, there's never enough dough."

"Then why do you keep having kids?" JJ asked.

"That's the question of the hour. We had trouble having the first kid. Now, all I do is look at the wife and she gets pregnant."

"So, quit looking at her, or take the initiative and make sure you're shooting blanks," Pat said.

"Look, I'm sorry if I caused you trouble at home," JJ said. He turned to look at Rick. "You should have said something. I could have found someone else to cover for me."

"Forget it, man. It's not only the over-time. It seems like nothing I do makes my wife happy lately."

"Trouble in paradise?" Pat asked.

"You might say that, or you might say she's losing patience being married to a cop."

"You should talk to Tom," JJ said. "He counsels cops on keeping their marriage together."

"I know, but I'm don't want to become his pet project of the month. In fact, I don't want anyone at the precinct to know I'm having problems at home. Let's just drop it and forget we had this conversation, okay?"

"Whatever you say, man, just trying to help," JJ answered. He turned his eyes back to the road.

"I don't need your help, or yours," Rick said, looking over his shoulder at Pat.

"I'm beginning to see why you're having trouble with your wife," she murmured.

"Something you need to learn besides policing, Rookie," Rick said.

"What's that?"

"To keep your nose out of things that don't concern you." Rick wadded his food wrapper and threw it in the empty bag.

"Or what?"

"Or you won't be around long enough to get past being a rookie."

* * *

When Pat returned to the precinct, Tom was waiting. He waved her in his office where she related her conversation with JJ and Rick.

"Rick's having problems at home. His wife resents his job and their financial situation. It could be a reason for him to look for a lucrative way to supplement his income or to get out of police work altogether."

She fidgeted. "And then, there's JJ."

Tom frowned. "What about JJ?"

Pat proceeded with caution, afraid Tom's history with the young officer might cloud his judgment. Tom had taken JJ under his wing when the cadet graduated from the Academy, looking out for him like a younger brother. The two cops were patrol-mates and had worked together on some major busts.

"He's missed shifts twice in the last month. He says he's been having stomach problems."

"It's not surprising since he's a junk-food addict."

"I checked with personnel. He never took a single sick day prior to your clamping down on the Kingpin the last several months."

"You're barking up the wrong tree," Tom said in a tone filled with displeasure, "but I'll look into it."

* * *

Tom found JJ pouring over paperwork at his desk. He leaned over the young man's shoulder.

"Having fun?" he asked.

"Sometimes, I think it's not worth making an arrest," JJ said, "with all the crappy reports we've got to do."

"You knew that when you signed on."

"Yeah, but it makes me feel better to spout off about it."

"You've probably got more than your share with your recent time off."

"You riding me about it, too?" Rick asked, looking at the lieutenant more closely. "I got a bellyful of it from Rick already."

"Bellyful is an apt description. He said you're having stomach problems. You got an ulcer?"

"The scumbags we arrest are enough to give anyone ulcers."

"No argument from me. Have you seen a doctor?"

"Naw, the pharmacist gave me something for it. It seems to be helping. Why are you so interested in my health?"

"Just looking out for a fellow officer," Tom said.

"Your concern is touching."

"I wouldn't want you getting sick out in the field when you're supposed to have my back."

"Don't worry. I've always had your back; I always will."

* * *

Tom saw Pat sitting at a table in the break-room. "Hope that's a fresh pot of joe."

"Brewed with my own hands," Pat said.

He pulled a mug from the cupboard and poured himself a cup. "I will say the coffee's been better since you arrived. The guys make it strong enough to choke a horse."

"I hope it's not the only improvement I've brought."

As he pulled out a chair, he leaned over and whispered. "You're reading things into JJ taking a couple of days off."

She kept her voice low. "You don't think there could be more to JJ's sick days than a stomach-ache?"

"Spit it out. What are you suggesting?" Tom asked. The sharpness in his voice surprised her.

"Mickey Flynn offered JJ a job as a dealer at the Card Club when the two of you questioned Mickey."

"Which JJ refused," Tom said.

"Have you considered JJ might have refused Mickey's offer because he was already working for Mickey's boss, the Kingpin himself?"

Tom's jaw clenched. Pat knew she was pushing the boundaries, but she pressed anyway. "You've taught me to search for reasons behind people's actions."

"What reason would JJ have for going to work for the Kingpin? He wants the scum behind bars as much as I do."

"Since I came on board, JJ's been riding with me instead of with you. Maybe he thinks it's a sign that he's not on the fast track in the division the way he thought he was. Maybe you two aren't as tight as you think."

"JJ knows why he's been riding with you the past couple of months. He's the best one for you to learn from, and he's someone you can relate to. He's a good cop, the kind you should model yourself after. If you were paying more attention to what you can learn from him, you might be doing your job better."

He threw his coffee dregs in the sink and stomped out of the kitchen.

Chapter Thirteen

Maddy parked in front of the main lodge an hour before she and Lea were scheduled to meet with the chief.

The Miller ranch was becoming one of Maddy's favorite places to be, and the handsome cowboy walking to greet her was becoming one of her favorite people to be with.

Scott took off his hat, running his fingers through unruly, curly hair. His face was chiseled and strong; his eyes dark and deep, like pools of chocolate filled with flecks of hazelnut. But to her, the dimples which dented his cheeks at the sight of her were his most endearing feature.

He opened her door and took her hand to help her out. His touch made a shiver run through her.

"Gramps told me you and your sister were coming to visit the chief today."

"I didn't expect to see you," she said, crossing her fingers behind her back. She had planned an early arrival in hopes of spending time with him. "Aren't you usually out at daybreak riding herd on your cows?"

His smile broadened. "Don't worry, Miguel and I have seen to the animals already. In case you hadn't noticed, it's hardly first thing in the morning."

"You country folks and us city folks operate in different time zones."

"It's not the only difference between us," Scott said, "but that's all right. It's differences that add spice to a relationship."

"Too much spice creates heartburn." Maddy shook out her sundress and flopped a wide-brimmed hat on her head.

"I reckon you've caused plenty of men heartburn."

She melted under his grin. "You aren't teasing me, are you?"

"Just enjoying you, Maddy, like I always do. Have you got time to see the new foal before Lea gets here?"

"Sure, I'd love to."

* * *

He rested his hand on her shoulder as they walked to the barn and pointed out a gaggle of baby geese toddling after their mother.

"They're adorable," Maddy said, snapping a picture with her phone camera.

At the corral, they saw a man brushing a baby horse; a filly with white markings on its lower legs and a star on its forehead.

"I'll bring her over to you," Scott told Maddy.

Unhooking the latch and closing the gate behind him, Scott walked slowly toward the filly. "How's she doing, Miguel?"

"She's a smart one, boss, just like her momma."

The young horse stood quietly to let Scott pet her forehead before she nudged the front of his shirt.

"See what I mean?" Miguel asked.

A smile spread across the face of both men as Scott reached into his pocket.

"Follow me, little one; you'll get your treat," he said, holding a baby carrot in the palm of his hand.

Maddy leaned over the top rail and stroked the horse's head as it nibbled the orange morsel.

Scott turned his back on the horse and walked away, calling over his shoulder. "C'mon, Lucky. Let's go."

The filly raised her head, turned, and followed the cowboy's lead around the corral.

"How does he do that?" Maddy asked the foreman when he joined her on the fence. "She's following Scott without him holding her with a rope."

"The boss has bonded with the filly. She trusts him; she knows she has nothing to fear. The horse enjoys spending time with him, so she's willing to follow his lead. In the next few days, he'll put a halter on to guide her."

"That's cool. The horse is doing what Scott asks of her own free will."

"It's the boss' way. He makes everything a partnership, a two-way venture, with animals just like with people."

Scott's grandfather joined them, leaning against the top rail. "Fun to watch, aren't they?"

"It seems to be the two of them in their own little world," Maddy said.

"My grandson's in the moment with the horse enjoying their time together. He does that with almost everything; stays in the moment. Most people are never present with what they're doing. They're thinking about something that happened the previous day or what they'll be doing tomorrow. They cheat themselves out of a good part of what's real in life by letting their mind carry them into fantasy worlds of daydreams or regrets."

"Is that something you taught Scott when he was growing up?"

"Everybody learns the importance of living in the moment in their own way; some through good advice, some through loss, some by simply being quiet long enough to listen to their inner voice. Sadly, many people never figure it out."

"Okay, Lucky, go play," Scott hollered. He gave the filly a gentle slap on the rump. The horse whinnied, and ran to join her mother and the other horses in the meadow.

They turned at the sound of tires crunching on the pebbled drive. A dog hung out of each back window of the approaching car.

"Thanks for suggesting my sister bring her dogs, Ralph," Maddy said. She gave Scott an explanation. "Lea's border collie has never had the experience of herding. I doubt she's ever seen a cow. We're anxious to see how Gracie reacts."

"You mean you want to see if the dog displays the herding instincts natural to her breed?" Scott asked.

"Isn't that what border collies do?"

Scott grinned. "Some bitches can't be typecast."

"If you're referring to me," Maddy said, "what can I say? I'd rather be someone's shot of whiskey than everyone's cup of tea."

"C'mon. Let's get your sister and the dogs sorted, and I'll walk you to the chief's house. You're in for a treat."

* * *

They walked beside a river reflecting shimmering sunlight. The dogs ran by their side and sniffed the underbrush as they shuffled through fallen leaves.

"I don't think I've ever heard so many birds in one place," Lea said.

Maddy stopped and listened to a high-pitched, screeching sound. She pointed to the tallest branch of a sycamore tree. "There it is, a red-tailed hawk."

"I didn't know you knew about birds," Lea said. She followed the line her sister's finger traced.

"Katie taught me."

"Kudos," Scott said, "you're a quick study."

"Talking about a quick study, I'd like to learn something about the chief before we meet him," Lea said. "How long has he lived on your ranch?"

"The chief's family were among the few remaining native tribes when my great-grandfather staked out the land."

"I know Chumash Indians have a history in this area," Lea said, "but I'll admit, I don't know much about them."

"In addition to being hunters and food-gatherers, they were boat-builders and fishermen. The Chumash were the supply source for clamshell beads used as money by most of the settlers. Over the years, millions of shell beads were made and traded from the offshore islands. Chumash artists were also known for weaving baskets and painting rocks."

"I always think of Indians in the olden days as living in tents," Maddy said. "Is that true?"

"The chief's ancestors lived in dome-shaped homes made of willow branches, whalebone, and netting. Light entered from a hole in the roof, and they built fires for cooking in the middle of the floor. He's told me as many as fifty people could live in one house.

"In places like this where food was easy to get, men and women had time for story-telling, music, and artwork. Each village had an area for ceremonies and dancing. They used flutes made of wood or bone, musical bows, and rattles."

"What happened to them?" Maddy asked, throwing a stick for Gracie. "You don't see many of them around these parts anymore."

"Spanish missions were established in Chumash territory in the eighteen-hundreds. They brought with them European diseases which all but destroyed the Indian population."

"How did the chief come to live with you?"

"The Miller ranch was carved out of a portion of the old Chumash territory. My ancestors hired many of the chief's tribe to work on the ranch. With the exception of the chief's forefathers, most of the Indians who lived on this land moved to a reservation.

"As the story goes, one of my fore-bearers had a gravely ill child. In current medicine, the body and mind are treated separately, but the Chumash Indians saw the spirit, mind, and body as inseparable entities which could not be treated separately in disease.

"One of the chief's ancestors mixed bark, roots, and flowers with animal fat. He painted it on the sick boy, but he also directed healing to the boy's mind and spirit. The child lived, so the chief's ancestor was asked to stay on the land to take care of the health and spiritual well-being of my relative's family."

"It's an interesting story," Lea said. "Do you think the chief has healing powers?"

"I'll let you decide for yourself."

Chapter Fourteen

As they turned from the fence-line and approached a clearing, two dogs came running toward them. Scott leaned over and stroked the dogs as they sniffed Gracie and Spirit.

"These are the chief's dogs, Tall-Grass and Running-Water."

When they rounded a bend and Scott pushed open a wooden gate, Maddy gasped. The corners of Scott's mouth turned up. "Were you expecting a dome-shaped hut made of willow branches?"

"I don't know what I was expecting," Maddy said of the picture-book setting, "but it wasn't this."

They crossed a small bridge over a bubbling stream which emptied into a pond filled with orange-and-black fish. The sweet smell of lavender, roses, and jasmine rose from both sides of the path. Twirling wind-chimes hung from the porch of a rambling ranch-style home.

The man who came down the walk to greet them had high cheek-bones, a bent nose, reddish-brown skin, and coarse, dark hair, streaked with gray. An Indian woman waited on the porch, drying her hands on an apron.

"Welcome," he said, grasping Maddy's hands in his own. "You're even lovelier than I remembered."

Maddy's face turned crimson as she glanced at Scott.

The chief turned to Lea. "And this must be your sister."

The kindness in his eyes and his gentle smile made Lea feel like he was someone she had known a long time.

"Come meet my wife and join us inside. Aponi has prepared some light refreshments."

"I'll leave you with him," Scott told Maddy and Lea. "I've got work to do. Why don't I take Gracie and Spirit to the barn with me? My dogs will show them what a working dog's day is all about."

"Great idea," Lea said. "They might learn something useful."

"Probably nothing they'll use at your house unless you need them to keep cows in line, but it might make them appreciate the pampering they get."

Gracie and Spirit followed Scott with eager anticipation as Lea and Maddy went to meet the chief's wife.

* * *

Years were etched into the woman's face like lines on a map. The hands which she reached out were veined like the tributaries of a river.

"You have a beautiful name," Lea told her.

"It means butterfly," the old woman said.

The chief's dogs stayed outside while the others entered a home furnished in modern and western styles which created an informal and gracious living environment.

Lea and Maddy sat on a couch while Aponi withdrew to the kitchen. The old man sat erect on a high-backed chair with his ankles crossed, and his arms folded across his chest.

"You have beautiful dogs, Lea. I can see that they are kind and wise spirit-guides."

"What do you mean, spirit-guides?" Maddy asked.

"There is a belief that animals possess souls and consciousness," the chief said, "and that they are here to teach humans. It's not a chance event which brings a dog or cat into our life. They come to teach us specific lessons. Spirit-guides walk through life with a person, teaching, guiding, and protecting them."

"Wow!" Maddy said, turning to Lea. "Did you know Gracie and Spirit were spirit-guides?"

"I've always felt they were more than four-legged animals. They seem to communicate with me but not the way humans do."

"You aren't saying they talk to you!"

"No, they communicate by touch and body movement, or even mental messages," Lea said. "Some people believe pets communicate with us in spirit even after they die."

"What do dogs teach us?" Maddy asked the chief, curious to hear more.

"They remind us that we're only a small part of creation. Each part has a place, and each creature has its own skill and wisdom. Animals have amazing powers but unlike humans, they only use their powers to benefit their kind, not to overcome their opponents."

"What powers do my dogs have?" Lea asked.

"Animals are said to have psychic gifts," the chief said. "Your dogs can tell your moods because they detect subtle energy frequencies which we can't. By watching and interacting with you, a dog anticipates how you're feeling and what you're going to do. It's part of their being a protector and a guardian."

"I never thought of dogs as being guides," Maddy said.

"Dogs can teach us a lot if we're open to learning from them. For one thing, they're faithful companions and enjoy being useful by serving us, but unlike humans who want to be rewarded and commended, dogs serve selflessly without needing their service to be praised."

"Gracie and Spirit always seem happy," Lea said, "and full of love."

"Dogs teach us the true meaning of unconditional love." The chief nodded, and his body swayed slightly back and forth. "Their sense of spirit and the ability to love, even when they're abused, is incredible. They show us how to give and receive love without imposing conditions or restrictions, and they carry the energy of forgiveness."

"Are dogs better spirit-guides than other animals?" Maddy asked.

"Possibly, because they understand humans, and they know the best way to guide us. They serve as a mirror image; in that way, they can be a great teacher."

"Are you saying they mirror our emotions?" Lea asked.

"Here's an example," the chief said. "If you encounter something when you're with Gracie which frightens you, she gets nervous and defensive, barking and circling around to protect you. If you're excited about going somewhere, she starts prancing and jumping to let you know she wants to go with you."

"That's exactly how she acts," Lea said, "but how does it teach me something?"

"What does Gracie do if you're upset or in a bad mood?"

"She comes to keep me company and remains quiet while I stroke her. It always makes me feel better."

"That's how she helps you out of your bad mood. One of the world's best-known stress relievers is petting a dog."

"It's true when I think about it," Lea said. "It's hard to stay in a self-absorbed pity party or feeling depressed when Gracie's waiting for me to play fetch."

"It's a dog's way of helping us move past our negative emotions and get over ourselves."

"I'll have to start paying more attention to Gracie and Spirit," Maddy decided. "What else can they teach me?"

"Animals spend their time being in the moment so they don't create suffering for themselves. They don't waste time worrying about what happened yesterday or what might be around the corner," the chief said, "and they don't carry a grudge like people do."

"Hold on a minute, Chief," Maddy said. She raised her eyebrows. "How can anyone know animals don't carry a grudge?"

"People who have studied animal packs find there's rarely a conflict between members of the pack because they solve their problems and move on. They seem to know by instinct that forgiveness gives us back our power. It helps us regain a sense of peace and allows us to get on with our lives.

"They also teach us to trust our intuition. Dogs are led by their instincts and they rely on gut reactions. We have these clues as well, but we don't always trust ourselves to follow our instincts."

"My sister's famous for her intuition," Maddy told the chief, patting her sister on the shoulder. "It's been the cause of her solving more than one crime."

The chief asked a question of his own. "What's your favorite thing about your dogs, Lea?"

"I love the way Gracie and Spirit show me how to see every day as being special. They're so excited when they wake up. They can't wait to find out what the day has to offer and they never feel short-changed with what they find. They start every day free of expectations and they don't require certain conditions be met in order to be happy."

"Animals don't worry if they'll be fed or if they'll receive what they want," the chief said, "and they don't spoil today's happiness by worrying whether tomorrow will be as good."

"Lea's dogs can't talk back, either," Maddy added, "and they don't require college tuition." They all laughed.

"You're right, chief," Lea said. "The love they give is free of terms and conditions. They don't demand mutually-beneficial exchanges. It's a love which expects nothing in return."

"An animal's unconditional love can be hard to understand for some people who are afraid to experience the enormity of universal love," the old man said. "Humans lack the knowingness of dogs that they are created worthy to be loved. They feel undeserving to receive unconditional love and loyalty. Conditioned by painful experiences, people are protective about exposing their true feelings.

"Dogs give their love without fear of being vulnerable. They accept love without worrying whether they could lose it again, and they don't look for ulterior motives when they're treated kindly."

"In many ways, they seem smarter than people about how to live," Lea said.

Aponi joined the conversation, placing a tray of vegetables, flat-breads, cheese, and hummus on the table. "I heard a story about a boy whose parents were trying to ease the pain of the impending euthanasia of their old beloved dog. Their veterinarian was talking to the child, explaining about life and death and what was about to happen.

"At one point, the young boy spoke up saying, 'It's okay, I know why we live longer than dogs. It's because it doesn't take them as long to learn the lessons God asks of them.'"

The chief smiled at his wife. "It's true; we're here to find and live our purpose. When we take the time to find out who we are and live according to our true purpose, we feel more fulfilled and our life becomes more meaningful."

* * *

"Which reminds me of our purpose in coming to see you," Maddy said. "We're hoping you can give us some history on the neighboring ranchers."

"Ralph knows the history as well as I do, but he says you need an impartial view."

"It could be relevant to a murder investigation Scott is involved in," Lea said.

"How can I help?" the Chief asked.

"There seem to be some seeds of contention among the ranchers."

"It's no secret the Millers and the Bensons disagree about the mustangs," the Chief said. "The Miller family brought charges against a rancher who was buying horses from the Bureau of Land Management and sending them to a slaughter house."

"Scott told me about the case," Lea said.

"What he probably didn't tell you is that Benson was suspected of being in cahoots with the rancher the Millers brought charges against. His participation couldn't be proved, so Albert wasn't included in the indictment."

The chief accepted a glass of lemonade from Aponi before continuing. "The other piece of history between the ranchers is the poker game which resulted in the Hudsons losing land to the Bensons."

"Our detective friend knows about that slice of folklore," Maddy told him.

"What's not common knowledge is that Benson's grandfather cheated at cards."

"Does Hudson know his grandfather lost the parcel in a crooked card game?" Lea asked.

"If he found out, it wasn't from the Millers. Ranchers leave well enough alone. They expect people to work out their own disputes."

"The general word is that Albert Benson was a hothead, constantly fighting with people. Is that how you would describe him?" Lea asked.

"Albert was not at peace. He was, indeed, a man in conflict."

"Who did he have his biggest conflict with?"

"The most dramatic conflicts are perhaps those which take place not between men, but between a man and himself."

"People say the man wasn't the same after his wife died," Lea said. "I met his wife once at an art course the city offered. She was the guest speaker at one of the classes and lectured on painting landscapes. You could tell by how much she loved her craft that she was a person who had found her true calling.

"I remember what a lovely woman she was. I'm sure losing her was terrible for both Albert and his son."

"The loss of a loved one is a life-changing event," the chief said. "For many, it's more than the loss, it's dealing with the feeling that the loss is unfair."

"How does a person cope?" Lea asked.

"I know of no way to find peace in loss other than to realize the greater wisdom to be gained, accepting that what we lose was meant to be lost whether it's a job, money, health, or love. For some people, it means being stripped of what's keeping them from learning. Those who resent the loss will never realize the gain which was intended for them."

Maddy couldn't help but think of Scott. "Surely there is nothing to be gained in the loss of a loved one. Think of how Scott and Katie suffered over the loss of his wife."

"It took a long time for Scott to move past the pain," the chief agreed, "more so, because he was unwilling to embrace it. White men are taught to cowboy up; if it hurts, don't show it. He was unable to accept that sometimes we end up exactly where we're meant to be, facing the challenges we're meant to face."

"How do we know what we're meant to learn?" Maddy asked.

"By trusting ourselves, something most people have forgotten how to do."

"In what ways are you saying people don't trust themselves?" Lea asked.

"They rely on schools to tell them how smart they are by measuring their intelligence with tests," the chief said. "They let employment agencies tell them which jobs will earn them the most money rather than bring them the most satisfaction. They buy a house on the right side of town, drive the latest model car, and let fashion magazines dictate how they should dress and cut their hair. They compare themselves to other people and try to measure up in terms of looks, wealth, and happiness.

"Most people find it easy to let other people tell them what to like or dislike, who to admire or disrespect, even who to love or hate. They avoid learning the lessons they were sent here to learn, afraid to find their own meaning, and to express who they truly are."

"My husband is right," Aponi said. She stood behind his chair and placed a hand on his shoulder. "People listen to their head instead of following their heart. They don't believe in themselves, so they can't accept how great they are. They never reach their potential because they won't let themselves be the person they were created to be. They feel undeserving, so they accept a life less than the life they deserve."

The chief nodded. "Many people lack the courage to claim their God-given right to a happy, abundant life because they've let the world around them convince them such a life is not possible; it's beyond their reach, dream-based, and not reality.

"They silence the voice inside to listen to the voices of pretenders, defeatists, and cynics. They create a persona to satisfy everyone around them, and end up dissatisfied."

"You're not anyone else's story but your own," Aponi said. She walked around the room, filling beverage glasses. "To model yourself on other people is like trying to catch a raindrop in your hand.

"The truth is that many people are living a dream, but it's a dream based on their limited vision of what they have a right to expect. They're like a caged bird who believes his life is within the bounds of the cage. Even when the door of the cage is opened, the bird fails to fly out to experience a bigger world."

"I've been there, I'm guilty of doing that sometimes," Lea admitted. "But why are people afraid to listen to their heart?"

"People have a thousand reasons, which aren't reasons but excuses," the chief said. "Maybe they're afraid to find out they're different than who they thought they were. Or, they're afraid to fail. What's wrong with failing? Society has attached a stigma to failure. If it weren't all right to fail, we wouldn't have been given the ability to dream."

"But who should we listen to?" Maddy asked. "Who has the right answers for us?"

"The answer is always in your heart," Aponi told her. "The problem is that we're so busy talking to other people, we don't listen to what's inside. We're incapable of sitting quietly by ourselves and letting answers flow to us."

"How do we know if something is the right thing for us to do?" Maddy persisted.

"It's not a matter of something being the right thing to do," the chief said. "You were created to be unique, like no one else on earth. When you understand your purpose here, you don't doubt anything which happens in your life.

"Something might seem good; it might seem bad. It might appear to be important, or insignificant. It may feel like the right thing to do, or it may feel wrong. None of that matters except that it has appeared in your life because it's part of your unique journey. It cannot be denied, nor should it be. It should be embraced and welcomed as the next higher step."

Lea asked a final question. "Why can't we do things better; why can't we be smarter, kinder, and less self-centered?"

"If we came here as the best version of ourselves, we wouldn't need to be here very long," the chief replied. His smile was as gentle as the bubbling stream under the bridge. "The longer we stay, the more opportunity we are given to step away from all the things we're not, until only who we are remains."

Chapter Fifteen

"The stuff the chief was talking about was cool, but I don't know if it got us closer to catching the murderer," Maddy said, as they followed the river back to the ranch.

"I'm not so sure," Lea said. "I think the chief was telling us that instead of looking for an obvious exterior motive, we should look at the inner conflicts these people were trying to resolve."

"Well, you're the thinker, I'm a doer. What should I be doing while you're pondering what the chief said?"

"Let's go for a hike," Lea suggested. "The dogs are with Scott. We have a chance to view the countryside."

"I'm all for exercise, but there could be snakes around here," Maddy pointed out.

"If you're thinking of letting your relationship with Scott develop, you better get used to snakes, lizards, spiders, and everything else that goes along with living in the country."

"Letting our relationship develop doesn't mean I'll end up living here," Maddy said, "although it would be an easy place to do some ever-aftering."

"Your problem is, you can't separate the vision of riding off into the sunset with a handsome cowboy and the realities of being a rancher's wife."

"Slow down. You're putting the cart before the horse. I haven't said anything about a future with Scott."

"You couldn't help but think about it. Keep in mind; he comes with a ready-made family."

"Let's focus on the moment," Maddy said, stomping off in the direction of the frontage road.

"Not that way. I want to go the back way across the Benson property to the Hudson ranch."

"You seem to know where you're headed. Have you got an agenda?"

"From what the chief said, it sounds like these neighbors have plenty of history; not all of it fond memories. It could provide the motive we're looking for. I need to wrap my head around who the other players are."

"I agree," Maddy said. "These ranchers had more than one bone to fight over. If they're stubborn like most cowboys, they're none too forgiving and prone to hold a grudge."

"Scott doesn't seem to be that way."

"He's not, but he's an exception," Maddy said. "In fact, he's exceptional any way you look at him."

"Watch out!" Lea shrieked. She grabbed Maddy's arm and backed away from the barking, snarling dog running toward them.

"Rascal," a boy's voice shouted.

The dog stopped dead in his tracks. The skin around his mouth stretched back to expose long, sharp teeth.

A second command echoed along the isolated riverbed. "Rascal, heel."

The voice giving the orders became visible when a youth of average height and brown hair came jogging toward them.

"He won't hurt you," the boy said. "You're on private property, the dog's only being protective."

Noting acne and the nervous shyness of a teen-ager, Lea reached out her hand. "You must be Dalton. I'm Lea Austin. This is my sister Maddy."

The dog's growl increased in volume as Lea moved toward his master. The boy picked up a stick and threw it toward the river. The dog scampered off to fetch it.

"How do you know who I am?" he asked, turning toward Lea. He narrowed his eyes and stared at her intently.

"We're friends of Scott Miller. We're guests at his ranch today, and he mentioned you and your sister. We were with Katie at the rodeo when—"

"Yeah, okay, I get the picture. What are you doing here?"

"Bird-watching," Maddy said. "Katie's been teaching me how to spot rare birds. She told me we might see a road-runner along this trail."

"Most bird-watchers have a camera," the boy said, looking them up and down.

"We were on our way back from meeting the chief," Lea responded. She hated to lie, but she didn't want him thinking they were spying on him. "We decided to go for a hike before Maddy could get the camera from her car. She's been taking pictures with her phone."

"I told my sister how mad I'll be if we're lucky enough to spot a rare bird, and I don't get a decent picture," Maddy said.

"You met the chief?" Dalton asked.

"Yes, he's an interesting man, and so wise," Lea said, relieved to move the conversation in another direction. "It must be great having him as a neighbor. If I lived close, I'd be pestering him with questions all the time."

The boy looked down and shuffled his feet. "Girls ask more questions than guys. We figure stuff out on our own."

Lea could sense unanswered questions hanging in the air, both hers and Dalton's. The dog interrupted the moment, dropping the stick at his master's feet.

"C'mon, Rascal. We've got work to do," the boy said. He turned away from the women.

Lea wanted to stop him so they could talk further, but she had no reason. He looked back before he and his dog moved out of sight. His eyes locked on hers.

"Nice meeting you," he said, barely loud enough to be heard.

* * *

"That was a close call!" Maddy said, catching her breath.

"With the dog or with Dalton figuring out we aren't bird-watchers?"

"Both, but were you impressed with my improvising?"

"If you mean shooting the breeze, that's genetic," Lea replied. "We both inherited that skill from Dad."

"Cops do have a tendency to expound on their adventures," Maddy agreed, "but it made for great bed-time stories."

Lea mused over the boy's behavior. "Do you think Dalton seemed nervous?"

"Maybe a bit skittish, but I can think of at least three good reasons for his acting that way."

"I'm listening," Lea said. She stopped walking and turned to her sister.

"First, his father's been killed. Second, we're strangers on his property."

"And third?"

"He's a teen-ager; their whole view of adults is skeptical."

"You could be right," Lea said. "Maybe we should head back."

"I thought you wanted to check out the neighbors, including the Hudson place."

"I'm a little skittish after our encounter with Dalton's dog," Lea admitted.

"You aren't going to let a show-down with a pair of canine fangs scare you off, are you?"

"You're the brave one," Lea said.

"C'mon, you can do it. Courage is being scared to death and saddling up anyway."

"That sounds like something Scott told you."

"Nope, John Wayne, but you remember Dad's version, don't you? Strength doesn't come from doing what you can do; it comes from doing what you thought you couldn't."

Lea glared at her sister. "You're a regular fountain of wisdom today."

"I guess it rubs off from being around the chief," Maddy said.

"All right, I'm game," Lea agreed, "but let's go back to the barn and get Gracie and Spirit. It's only five minutes from here. I'll feel safer with them along."

* * *

Things at the Hudson ranch seemed quiet enough, but the women spoke in whispers.

"I don't see anyone. Let's check it out," Maddy said, pointing toward the barn. Lea gave a thumbs-up.

The sisters advanced, crouching and stepping gingerly on dried leaves and sticks.

As they moved past a corral, a horse raised its head and pawed the dirt. A chicken scurried out in front of them.

Lea put a finger to her lips to warn Spirit and Gracie, but it was too late. The dogs took off, chasing the chicken toward the barn.

The women ran after them, splitting up to search each side of the building for the dogs.

"Psst," Maddy hissed moments later, motioning for her sister. "Come take a look."

Lea crossed to a fenced storage area where she found Maddy snapping pictures.

"What did you find?"

"You mean what did Gracie find? Luckily, I pulled her away before she put her nose where it didn't belong."

"What is it?"

"Something I think Tom will be plenty interested in seeing," Maddy said, as they stood side by side staring at four black canisters labeled with cross-bones.

* * *

A voice boomed behind them. They both jumped. "What do you two think you're doing?"

They spun around, coming face-to-face with a man fitting Tom's description of Cliff Hudson.

"My sister and I were bird-watching," Lea said, too quickly. "My dogs ran in here after a chicken."

"You call it bird-watching and chasing chickens, I call it trespassing," he growled.

"We didn't think about being on private property," Maddy said. "Sorry, I guess we got carried away."

"I don't know what you city folks do about trespassers, but out here in the country, we shoot 'em," he said, spitting out a wad of chewing tobacco big enough to make Lea's stomach churn.

126

He pulled a gun out of a holster strapped around his waist, twirling it around on his finger before pointing it at them.

Maddy handled her cell phone as smartly as the rancher handled his gun. Hitting speed dial, she glared at him.

"I'm calling my detective friend. If you're going to shoot us, I want him to know exactly what happened here. Wouldn't want you ruining my good name if I'm no longer around to defend myself."

"What the blazes are you doing, missy?" shouted Hudson, taking a step toward her.

"Hey, Tom. I only have a minute. I'm about to be shot by—"

She held the phone away from her ear and pressed the speaker button. "What's your name, mister?"

"Put the phone down," Hudson ordered.

"He won't give me his name, but it's the ranch next to the Benson farm. We're in the man's barn. Regardless of what he might tell you when you find our bodies, my sister and I were bird-watching and wandered onto his property by mistake."

"Geez, Maddy, what have you gotten yourself into?" Tom demanded. "Is this a joke?"

"Not by the looks of the pistol this dude's pointing at us."

"Dang blast it. I'm on my way, but this better not be—"

Maddy clicked off.

She put an arm around Lea's shoulder. "Detective Elliot is on his way. If this guy shoots us, he'll have a lot of explaining to do."

They both held their breath as they watched Cliff Hudson holster his gun.

* * *

Tom sped up the driveway. "Crap," he cursed, hitting a pot-hole big enough to elevate him a foot off the front seat.

He leaped out of the car, running toward the barn. "Maddy, you in there?"

"Come on in."

Her voice sounded too calm for someone whose life was being threatened.

He used caution entering the building but let out his breath when he saw the sisters sitting comfortably on a bale of hay. Gracie stood watch over a mound on the floor which was emitting a stream of rambling profanity.

The object of the dog's attention was Clifford Hudson, arms and legs trussed like a chicken.

Tom loosened the ropes and hoisted the rancher onto his feet.

"This man was threatening to shoot us," Maddy said. "We had to subdue him in self-defense."

"These bitches were trespassing," Hudson sputtered.

"I'll sort this out with you at headquarters. Right now," Tom said, turning to the sisters and pointing toward the road, "I want you two and the dogs out of here. Wherever your car is, you need to be in it within the next two minutes and on your way back to town."

Lea grabbed Tom's arm. "Hold on. There's something you need to see."

Hudson stepped forward, but Tom signaled him to stay put and followed Lea toward a storage area.

She pointed to the cans marked poison. "I think we found the culprit poisoning Benson's crops."

"I have no way to use this as evidence. I can't get a warrant to search the property without cause."

"We've given you cause," Maddy said, "he threatened Lea and me."

"He's going to say you were trespassing. He has a right to protect his property."

"You can use the excuse that you believe there may be other weapons on the property," Lea suggested.

"I suppose I can do that if he can't produce proper registration for the gun he used to threaten you," Tom said. "By the way, tit for tat. I've set up protection for Amber at the hospital."

"Thanks, Tom, that will help me sleep better tonight."

"Before you leave," Maddy said, anger rising, "you might take a closer look at the pistol this guy was shoving in our faces. I'm no expert on guns, but it looks like Scott's, the one you're calling the murder weapon."

"How did you disarm him?" Tom asked, pushing Hudson in front of him.

Maddy's eyes glistened with pride.

"I had a little help," she said, stroking Gracie's head, "but do you think I take self-defense classes for my amusement?"

"I've seen you throw your trainer to the mat a few times. You looked to me like you were enjoying yourself."

"I'll admit I enjoy getting the better of a man," she said.

"Remind me never to underestimate you again," Tom told her.

"I will, and you can stop worrying about protecting me."

"Doubt I'll ever be able to do that."

* * *

The sisters walked to the Miller ranch for their cars. Scott walked toward them while Lea was loading the dogs. Maddy talked rapidly, excited to tell him about their talk with the chief and their adventure at the Hudson ranch.

"Why didn't you call me when Cliff caught you? I would have come over and straightened him out in a hurry."

"We handled ourselves just fine," Maddy bragged.

"A real cowgirl can do it all by herself," Scott said. A grin spread across his face. "But a real cowboy won't let her."

"We called Tom because we found evidence he needed to see," Lea said. "Do you think Cliff is capable of poisoning Albert's crops and livestock?"

"He's capable, all right, he and every other farmer who has to deal with rodents, insects, and snakes, but I don't know if he'd stoop to destroying another man's livelihood."

"He might have done it to force Albert's hand over the sale of his land," Lea said. "Money makes men do things they wouldn't normally do."

"If that was Cliff's intent, he didn't know Albert as well as I thought he did. If Albert found out someone was trying to sabotage him, he'd only dig in his heels."

"Forget about that," Maddy said, turning to Scott. "Thanks for letting us meet the chief. Talking to him was great. I only wish—"

"Tom could have been here," Scott said.

Maddy's hand flew to her mouth. "How do you read my thoughts?"

"Don't worry; it's all right. I'm not in competition with Tom. That's not how I look at things."

She sighed with relief. "He probably won't come while you're topping his list of suspects, but I wish he would. Even the great wise detective could learn a thing or two from the chief."

"He's welcome anytime," Scott said.

Maddy touched Scott's arm. "You're such a great guy, I don't deserve you as a friend."

"Didn't you learn anything from the chief about what we think we deserve?" Lea said. They all laughed as Lea pulled out her keys. "Thanks, Scott. It's been enlightening; all of it, including our discovery in Hudson's barn."

"What's your next move, Sis?"

"I'm going to the Benson place tomorrow to talk to Dalton. He seemed overly distraught when we ran into him. I have a feeling there's something he's not telling Tom."

"Go for it," Maddy said. "I'm the biggest fan of your intuition."

"Nice to have the vote of confidence, but I didn't need it. I would have gone without your blessing."

"Don't I know it."

* * *

Scott walked Maddy to her car. Lea backed out and waved as she drove past.

The cowboy took off his hat, leaned through Maddy's open window, and kissed her. "I'm glad you're safe."

He replaced his hat, stuffed his hands in his back pockets, and strolled up the hill.

Maddy rolled down the rest of the windows and fanned her face to cool the heat climbing up her neck. A buzz on her phone drew her attention to a text from Lea.

'If a man takes off his hat to kiss you, he's a keeper. Have you found your knight in shining armor?'

Maddy texted back. 'Forget a knight in shining armor. A guy in blue jeans will do just fine.'

Chapter Sixteen

The next morning, Lea turned off the frontage road and parked her car in front of a farmhouse with a manicured yard which felt strangely familiar. Looking toward the barn, she realized her error. She was rapidly retracing her steps when a woman's voice stopped her.

"Can I help you?"

"I'm looking for the Benson farm."

"You've come to the Hudson ranch, I'm Mildred Hudson. The Bensons are the next farm up the road, but I don't think anyone's home. I can call if you like, save you a wasted trip if no one's there."

"Thanks, but that's not necessary," Lea said, looking for Cliff Hudson. She was anxious to leave. Beads of perspiration appeared above her lip.

"You look hot. Come in while I make the call. I'll fix you a lemonade."

"I don't want to take your time," Lea said, glancing over her shoulder.

"My husband's gone to town so I can take a break. I'd enjoy a cool drink myself." She held the screen door open. "I didn't catch your name."

Lea relaxed and followed the woman inside. She offered her first name but not her last. No sense giving more information than was needed.

"Make yourself comfortable. I'll be right back."

Lea walked around the room, and stopped in front of a framed painting above the fireplace. The sound of ice cubes clinking against the side of a pitcher made her jump.

"Do you like landscapes?" the woman asked.

"This one is beautiful. It's a Victoria Benson original, isn't it?"

"My husband bought it, which is almost a joke," Mildred said, handing Lea a glass, "because Clifford's idea of art is having his picture taken at Sears. I think he liked bragging that we had a famous artist for a neighbor. I've never felt it goes with our decor."

"It's lovely."

Mildred touched the icy glass to her forehead and gazed absently at the painting. "Landscapes aren't my thing. I prefer flowers you can put in a vase and smell instead of pictures of them hanging on a wall."

She turned back to Lea. "There was no answer at the Benson place, but I can call again later."

"I'll work it out, but I appreciate your trying."

"I haven't seen you around these parts before," Mildred said. "Do you visit the Bensons often?"

Lea squirmed, feeling the woman's scrutiny of her tailored trousers and ankle-high boots, fashionable but hardly ranch attire. She wondered if her husband had described the women he caught in his barn.

"I'm afraid I met Lucy under the worst possible conditions. I was at the rodeo when her father was found murdered. I'm anxious to find out how she's doing."

"Terrible thing," Mildred said, shaking her head, "them being our neighbors and all. Clifford had looked for Albert not long before the body was discovered. It would have been better if he'd found Albert instead of that poor girl. It will stick with Lucy the rest of her life.

"As far as I know, she's back in school. She spent a couple of days with the Millers, but she wanted to get back to her classmates."

"How's the son doing?" Lea asked.

"He's got his hands full. I don't know how he'll be able to continue night classes now that there's only him to run the farm."

"You must have known Albert well."

"As well as any of us know anyone, I imagine."

"Were you close to his wife before she passed?"

"Not really," Mildred said, "we were different types. Victoria was an artist, and I'm a rancher's wife. There's a world of difference in the way we see things. Albert and I probably had more in common, but he admired his wife's talent. He held that woman on a pedestal."

"So your husband was at the rodeo Sunday as a contestant?" Lea couldn't imagine a man as large as Clifford bouncing around on a bull.

"Heaven's, no; he's a judge. I've never understood what he gets out of officiating at those cowboy events. I'd rather he'd judge the barbecue cook-off. I'd win every time with my rib sandwiches, his favorite.

"Speaking of that man, excuse me for a moment. I'm going to give him a call. He should have been home an hour ago."

Lea's heart skipped a beat. She jumped to her feet. "I've got to be going. I enjoyed meeting you."

"You don't want to stay to meet Clifford?"

"Another time."

The last thing she wanted was to explain to him for a second time what she was doing on his property.

* * *

Lea heard barking when she pulled into the next drive up the road. The dog she and Maddy had encountered on their way to the Hudson ranch came running around the corner of the house. This time she was prepared.

She opened the glove compartment and pulled out a baggie filled with dog treats. She threw some as far as she could and watched the dog scamper after them before getting out of her car.

"Hello, anyone home?" she called, knocking on the screen door. There was no response.

The dog raced to the back yard. Lea followed and found the young man weeding a vegetable garden.

"Hi, Dalton," Lea said. The boy swirled around, dropping a weed puller from his hand.

"What are you doing here?" he asked, wiping a dirty hand on the back of his jeans.

"We didn't get a chance to talk yesterday. I stopped by to see if you and your sister need any help. I brought some brownies. If you're anything like my son, you forget to eat."

Dalton's face relaxed. He pulled the bandanna from his neck to wipe sweat from his forehead. "The neighbors have been bringing food. We've got plenty."

"How are you getting along?" Lea asked, setting the plastic container on a table.

"Lucy and I are doing fine." His jaw jutted out. He raised himself to his full height.

The dog sniffed at the brownies. "Mind if I give your dog a treat?" Lea asked, reaching into her pocket. "Rascal, is that his name?"

The dog looked to the boy the way a child looks at a parent for permission.

"Go ahead," Dalton said, tossing his hair away from his eyes, "but make him beg for the treat."

Lea gave the command she used with her dogs. "Sit."

The dog obeyed, waiting eagerly for more instructions. "Shake. C'mon, paw up. Good boy."

Lea opened her hand and looked at Dalton. "You've trained him well."

"Dad trained him. He never let the dog have anything without doing something for it. Before Rascal got fed in the morning, he had to round up the chickens so Lucy could fetch eggs. By the time he got fed at night, he'd spent the whole day running after the tractor, swimming in water troughs, and keeping the cows in line.

"Dad used to say the smart ones are better company and harder workers than a hired hand." Dalton grinned, pulling off his gloves. "And they drink less alcohol, and tear up fewer trucks."

Lea looked around. "Looks like you're doing most of the work. Do you have hired help?"

"Nope, it's just me and my sister now." He crossed his arms in front of his chest trying to look bigger than he was.

"Is there—"

"Thanks for stopping." He turned his back on her. "I've got to get back to work."

Lea wanted to keep the conversation going. "Could I bother you for a glass of water?"

Dalton's head jerked around. His eyes were wide like he'd been caught doing something wrong. "Sorry, I'm forgetting my manners. I should have asked."

He grabbed the container of brownies and headed for the house.

"No problem, Lea said, following him. "I appreciate it."

* * *

The house was small and dark. Lea was tempted to move from window to window throwing open the curtains to let in the sunshine. Plates encrusted with dried food sat on the coffee table. Sweaters were strewn on the couch and chairs. The charred remains of burned logs formed piles of soot in the fireplace. The room was in need of a thorough dusting and mopping.

Dalton saw her eyes sweeping over the living room as they walked through to the kitchen. "I take care of everything outside the house, the inside is Lucy's job. She hasn't been able to get her head around it the last few days."

"Totally understandable. How is she doing?"

"She took a couple of sick days. She's been spending time with the Millers."

"She was upset with Scott Miller after what happened at the rodeo," Lea recalled. "I heard her tell him she never wanted to see his family again."

"She got over that in a hurry. She didn't want to stay here Sunday night. Neither did I. We were glad to have somewhere else to go."

"Today was my sister's first day back at school," Dalton said, removing a pitcher of water from the refrigerator. "Katie and her dad picked Lucy up this morning to make sure she'd be all right about seeing the other kids at school."

"And is she—"

"Okay about what happened?" Dalton responded in an acid tone. "How all right can a twelve-year-old be about her old man being shot?"

"I'm sorry, Dalton," Lea said, "truly sorry, for you and your sister."

"Yeah, well, stuff happens. Life goes on. Lucy will get over it."

Lea noted the emotional shifts Dalton made between being a young boy and being mature beyond his years. She hoped his latest experience wouldn't lead to his becoming a bitter man like his father.

She set the glass down and took a step toward him. He backed up against the sink.

Placing a hand gently on his shoulder, she lifted his chin with her other hand so she could look into his eyes. "Most people your age haven't lost both their parents."

Neither of them moved for several moments. Lea heard the wall clock ticking and water dripping from the faucet.

The boy's eyes teared before his head dropped to his chin. His shoulders sagged as his body started to shake.

"How will Lucy ever get over it?" he moaned. "She's all alone now."

"She has you, Dalton, she loves you. She looks up to you like a parent. She knows you'll take care of her."

Dalton threw her hand from his shoulder. He turned toward the sink and gripped the basin.

He spoke so softly, Lea could barely hear him. "How will she feel when she finds out what happened?"

"What do you mean?"

He spun around, fire replacing the tears in his eyes. "Will she love me when she knows I killed her father?"

* * *

Lea would remember the moment forever; she and Dalton standing inches apart, staring at each other. There was smoldering emotion in Dalton's eyes, but not the kind which made Lea feel threatened. It was more pain than anger.

She dropped into one of the chairs at the kitchen table and pointed to the other.

"Sit down, Dalton," she said, with enough authority to make the boy obey. "Tell me what happened."

The boy flung himself onto the chair, slamming his elbows on the table, and holding his head in his hands.

"We went to the fairgrounds early Sunday morning. Dad took care of the registration while I helped Lucy get her horse ready. When we finished, she went to the trailer and came back dressed in her riding gear.

"Dad had bought my sister a new pink-and-black shirt and a vest with white tassels. She looked real pretty." Pride flickered in his eyes. "There was time before the contest. She went to find Katie to show off her new duds."

"Did your father see her in her new outfit?"

"Nope, he'd already started his pre-contest ritual."

"Ritual?"

"He'd fill a canteen with booze and throw back a couple of drinks before every competition. Nerves, I suppose. When Lucy won, he'd treat us to burgers at the concession stand. If she lost, he'd walk over to the beach, sit on a rock, and keep tipping that canteen back until it was empty. Then he'd stumble to the trailer and I'd drive us home."

"What happened Sunday before the competition?"

"When it neared time to get Lucy to the arena, I went to the Millers' trailer looking for him."

"Was Scott at the trailer?"

"Nobody was there." He stared out the window. His voice took on an icy tone which sent a shiver up Lea's spine. "I saw my chance."

"Your chance for what?" Lea asked, afraid to hear the answer.

"To get a gun."

"Why did you want a gun?"

"To make my dad listen to me. I'd tried talking to him before but he never heard what I was telling him."

"Did you get Scott's gun?"

"Yeah, the one he uses in the shooting competition. He keeps it locked in a case, but I know where he hides the key because I clean his guns for him."

"What did you want to discuss with your father?"

"We needed to talk about the ranch. He was being unreasonable."

"Unreasonable how?" Lea asked.

"We had an offer to sell. Dad wasn't even willing to consider it.

"We'd argued before about money for tuition. Dad never gave me a cent, I earned every penny myself. Dad didn't believe in a college education. He wanted me to get a full-time job or work the ranch with him, but I can't take living on the farm anymore."

"Your mother was famous for her landscapes. I would think love of the land comes naturally to you."

"I grew up loving it as much as my parents did. My father loved the land for what it produced; my mother loved the land for its beauty.

"But things have changed since her passing. Trying to keep this run-down place going is killing me. I can't help with the farm, earn tuition money working at the Miller ranch, and go to college, too."

"I've been told you're a great help to the Millers," Lea said.

"I like working for them. They always tell me how smart I am and what a great job I do, words I never heard from my Dad.

"But I have no future in ranching. If I don't break away, I can't make a different life for myself. I figured if Dad sold the place, he'd give me the money I need for college. We could all move to town."

"Does Lucy share your feelings?"

"Lucy doesn't know what's best for her. She feels okay about living out here because it's all she's ever known, but she'd be better off being closer to her friends at school. She'd have more opportunity to participate in sports and after-school activities. Besides, Dad hasn't had much interest in the place since Mom died. I thought it would be good for him to get a fresh start, too."

"So you thought waving a gun in his face would make him listen?"

"Stupid, huh?" Dalton said. Red color flooded his cheeks. "Everybody knows you can't get my dad to listen, but I wasn't willing to fight him like most guys. I didn't want to hurt him."

"And did your father listen?"

"The bonehead was too wasted to hear a word I was saying. He was weaving all over the place. I was wasting my breath."

"Did you mean to shoot him, Dalton?"

"Heck, no. I was swinging my arms around, yelling at him to pull himself together before Lucy's competition started. I didn't want him embarrassing her like he'd done before, sitting in the stands drunk, yelling obscenities at the judges and other competitors.

"The next thing I knew, the gun went off. Dad staggered, then he fell."

A knot formed in Lea's chest as she felt the weight of that terrible moment. "Did you try to help him?"

"He was lying there curled up in a ball like a baby. I panicked. I dropped the gun and ran."

"Where did you go?"

"I was out of my head. I went to the bike path beside the river and started running. I ran for miles until my lungs burned and my shirt was soaked. It felt like I'd run to the ends of the earth.

"When I leaned over to catch my breath, I looked around and saw I'd run all the way home. I went inside and sat on the couch in the dark until Scott Miller came to tell me my father was dead. He took me to his place to spend the night."

The only sound was the swinging pendulum of the grandfather clock; ticktock, ticktock.

"Listen to me, Dalton." She moved over to put an arm around the boy's shoulder, but spoke with a firm voice. "You need to tell Detective Elliot what you've told me."

"I can't," he sobbed. "I'll go to prison. What will happen to Lucy?"

"You didn't shoot your father on purpose, you had no intent to kill him. The important thing is to turn yourself in. Tom and I will do everything we can to help you, I promise."

She tapped a number on her phone. Dalton jumped up and ran out the door.

Lea leaped up to chase him. The screen door banged in her face.

She saw Dalton leap into his truck and heard the sound of a revving engine.

"Dalton, don't run," Lea screamed at the speeding vehicle. "Stop, please stop."

She choked on a cloud of dust and felt the sting of flying pebbles on her cheek.

The watched the vehicle slow at the gate and then turn toward the Miller ranch.

* * *

The tires of Lea's car screeched as she rounded the frontage road at full-speed. She heard a voice squawking and picked up her phone from the dashboard where she'd thrown it.

"I hear you, Tom. Dalton Benson just confessed to me that he shot his father."

"What the blazes! Where are you?"

"I was at the Benson place, but Dalton bolted. I'm following him. It looks like he's headed for the Miller ranch."

"I'm on my way. Give me the description of the vehicle he's driving. I'll put out an all-points bulletin."

"Please, don't. He's not running; he's frightened. Cops chasing him with sirens blaring will put him in panic mode. I'll let the Millers know to watch for him. I'm sure we'll find him."

"All right, but don't do anything stupid before I get there. Scared people do crazy things."

"I'll be careful."

Chapter Seventeen

Lea ran into the Main lodge as soon as she arrived at the Miller ranch.

"Is anybody here?" she called out, her eyes darting around the room.

The door to the kitchen swung open, and Ralph Miller walked in.

"Hello, Lea. What a nice surprise," he said, before noting the worried look on her face. "What's wrong? Has something happened to my grandson?"

"No, it's Dalton Benson. I was just visiting him at their farm. He told me he took Scott's gun and shot his father."

The older man's jaw slackened, his face paled, and he grabbed a chair for support. "I don't believe it."

"It's true. Dalton was trying to talk to his father about selling the ranch. Albert was drunk. He wouldn't listen. Dalton got upset and shot him."

Ralph stood up straight. "Dalton couldn't have fired the shot that killed his father. The boy can't hit the broad side of a barn."

"What are you saying?" Lea asked.

"He's near-sighted, but too vain to wear glasses. I took him hunting once to teach him to shoot. It was hopeless. He couldn't have hit anything smaller than an elephant. We gave up after one trip."

"He said he didn't mean to shoot," Lea said. "He was yelling and waving his arms around. The gun discharged. When he saw his dad fall, he panicked and ran."

"Where is he now?"

"I don't know. I wanted him to talk to Detective Elliot. I told him we'd help him. But when I dialed Tom's number, Dalton ran out the door.

"He headed this way. We need to find out if anyone's seen him." Lea paced, wringing her hands. "What about his truck? Is it anywhere around?"

Ralph stepped onto the front porch and fired a flare. "That will bring all the hands running. If he's anywhere on the property, we'll find him."

"Tell them to be careful," Lea warned. "He's desperate. We need to approach him with caution."

"Don't worry, I'll make sure no one gets hurt. Sit tight while I tell the men what to do," he said, leaving her alone.

There must be something I can do, Lea thought. Where would he go? Where can he hide?

She raced to her car and sped back to the Benson place.

* * *

When Tom arrived at the Miller ranch, he saw men fanned out in every direction calling Dalton's name. He headed for the lodge where he found Ralph Miller barking out directions.

"Any sign of the boy?" Tom asked.

"Not so far, but we'll find him."

"Were you surprised to learn of his confession?"

"Shocked and disbelieving is more like it. The boy couldn't have done it. I've known him his entire life, he's not capable of such an act."

"Lea told me what you said about him being near-sighted."

"Poor eyesight wasn't the only reason the boy wouldn't go hunting. He refused to kill any living thing, including rabbits or squirrels. He inherited the gentle nature of his mother, not his father's survival skills. The notion the boy is a murderer is ludicrous."

Scott approached, followed by two of his ranch hands.

"Anything?" his grandfather asked.

"Nothing."

Tom faced Scott. "A couple of quick questions, if you don't mind."

"Really, Detective!" Ralph said. "Can't you find a better time to harass my grandson?"

"I wouldn't be asking if it wasn't important."

Tom's questions had barely been asked and answered when he got a text from Lea.

Reading the message, he turned to Scott, urgency in his voice. "Lea's found the boy. Where's the sweat lodge?"

"I'll take you," Scott said.

Ralph grabbed Tom's sleeve. "Are you going to arrest Dalton?"

"I agree the boy didn't kill his father but not for the reasons you've given. I'll explain later. Right now, I need to hear what he has to say."

* * *

The two men jumped into Scott's jeep and sped up a back road along the river. Tom held tightly to the door frame. His teeth jarred as they drove over potholes. "So what's a sweat lodge?"

"It's a place where purification ceremonies are done."

"Clue me in. What's the purpose of this so-called purification?"

"The sweat is a religious ceremony intended for prayer and healing. The aim of the ritual is to purify one's mind, body, spirit, and heart. Because the sweat lodge is dark, hot, and moist, it represents returning to the womb and the innocence of childhood."

"Who leads the ceremony?"

"It can only be led by elders who know the language and traditions. There's a Chumash Indian chief living here. He conducts them."

"What's done during the ceremony?"

"Water is poured over heated rocks. It goes up in steam and fills the air. At that moment, the participants are connecting themselves to the basic elements of life which bring out the greatest good in people. It's not only a way to cleanse but to release anger, guilt, and shame in a safe way."

"Sounds like a place where a kid who thinks he's murdered his father might want to hang out."

* * *

Scott pulled the jeep to a stop in front of a dome-shaped structure no more than four feet high. It was constructed of saplings and covered with blankets.

Leaving the vehicle, Tom observed burning logs in an area a short distance away.

"That's where a fire is built and the stones are heated," Scott said. "When the stones are white hot, they are taken into the lodge."

He stopped when they reached the structure.

"Let's go," Tom ordered.

"The flap has been dropped over the door. The ceremony has started, no one is allowed in."

"I don't mean to be disrespectful," Tom said, "but I've got to get in there. I'm going to have to crash this little party."

"Likewise meaning no disrespect, Detective, but participating in a purification ceremony might not be a bad idea for you."

"Some other time. Right now, I've got a murder to solve."

Crawling into the lodge, they were engulfed by darkness except for a fiery red glow in a shallow pit in the center of the room.

A shiver ran up Tom's spine. "What's that?" he whispered, pointing to a buffalo skull on top of a post.

"Don't worry," Scott said. "There are no shrunken heads here. It's only a barrier to warn of the hot stones. It keeps tall guys like you from falling into the fire."

"Believe me, I'm not about to get close enough to fall in," Tom said, staring at the feathers on an altar at the base of the post.

As his eyes adjusted to the darkness, he made out the forms of two people sitting cross-legged against the wall of the lodge. An Indian chief sat across the fire smoking a peace pipe.

Tom moved on hands and knees toward what he recognized as Lea's long copper hair. He crossed his legs and squatted, shifting uncomfortably on the mat of cedar boughs covering the floor.

The chief dipped water and poured it onto the hot stones in the pit, producing large clouds of steam.

Beads of sweat streamed down Tom's face. "This place is like a steam bath," he complained.

"That's sort of the point," Scott said.

The detective leaned across Lea to touch Dalton's shoulder. The young man appeared to be in a trance, unaware of his surroundings. His face was a mask of serenity, empty of signs of fear or anxiety.

He turned his head. His hooded eyes appeared unfocused but calm.

"Are you here to arrest me for murdering my father?" His voice was strangely steady with a flat tone of hopelessness which sent a wave of pity through the detective.

"I beg you, Tom," Lea pleaded. "This boy is not a murderer."

"Lea's right, son. The shot you discharged didn't kill your father. It was a blank."

Lea gasped, covering Dalton's hand with her own. "What's happened, have you found new evidence?"

Tom spoke directly to Lea, uncertain the boy was taking in what was being said. "When I saw Maddy last night, she told me I needed to look at things differently. I applied her advice to this case. Instead of trying to prove Scott guilty, I changed my point of view to prove he's innocent.

"I sent my sergeant back to the crime scene where he found a second casing. I checked the coroner's report. There was only one bullet in the body, the one which pierced the victim's heart.

"The sergeant looked everywhere, but there was no second bullet to be found. When he examined the metal casing, he noted it was crimped on the end; the kind used when the sound and flash of gunfire is needed, but a projectile would not be safe, like the cartridges used in—"

"Cowboy mounted shooting," Lea said, her excitement growing.

"The crucial element was the timing," Tom continued. "Dalton helped his sister get ready for her event. His father took care of the registration which meant Dalton didn't get a program of events. Before I got your text, I confirmed with Scott the scheduling of the shooting event and when he loaded his gun with blanks. What Dalton didn't realize when he took Scott's gun was that Scott had already prepared the gun for the contest."

"Which means the live rounds had been replaced with blanks," Lea said.

"That's correct. When Dalton accosted his father, the gun he was using couldn't have killed anyone."

"He fired a blank," Lea concluded, relief flooding her face. "But what made Dalton think he'd killed his father?"

"He saw his father fall to the ground, but that may have been caused by Albert being startled at the sound of the shot or the result of his drinking."

"You mean when Dalton's gun went off and Benson fell down, Albert wasn't dead, he was only dead-drunk," Scott said. "But if there were two cartridges, how do you explain there being only one gun at the scene, namely, mine?"

Tom offered an explanation, waving his hand in front of his face to ward off the vapors engulfing the room.

"The way I see it, someone was on their way to take care of Albert. When they arrived at Benson's trailer, they heard Dalton arguing with his father. They saw the flash of smoke when the kid fired the blank."

"They watched Dalton drop the gun and run off," Lea said, putting the pieces together. "When they saw Albert moving around, they realized a perfect opportunity to accomplish their dastardly deed and blame it on his son."

"All they had to do was pick up the gun Dalton dropped, reload it with live ammunition, walk over to Benson and shoot him," Tom concluded. "The bullet the murderer used was real and fatal."

"If there were two shooters, there should have been two sets of prints on the gun," Lea reasoned.

"No such luck," Tom informed her. "It would make things a whole lot easier to prove, but the gun was wiped clean."

"Even before you got Lea's call," Scott guessed, "you'd figured out the murderer wasn't Dalton."

"When I reviewed the coroner's report on the angle of the bullet," Tom said, "it indicated the person firing the shot was standing over the victim."

"Meaning the victim was already on the ground," Lea said.

"The fatal bullet was fired after Dalton had fled the scene."

"What are you going to do, Tom, are you going to arrest the boy?" Lea asked. "An attorney could claim Dalton had knowledge the gun contained blanks which would indicate his intent in waving the gun around was harmless."

"I can charge him with brandishing a weapon, but that's a misdemeanor. He'd serve minimum time in county jail." Tom brushed aside further supposition. "I'm not interested in pursuing the kid. The only person I'm interested in now is the one who put a live round in the gun. Who else at the rodeo had reason to want Albert out of the way?"

Lea turned to Dalton. "You can help find that person. I need you to remember every detail from when you got hold of Scott's gun until the gun went off and you ran."

Dalton leaned back against the wall and closed his eyes. "The only person I remember seeing was Mr. Hudson. He saw me with Scott's pistol. I remember his exact words to me: 'What the sam hill do you think you're doing?' I told him, 'Get out of my way. I need to talk some sense in my dad's head so he'll sell the ranch.'"

"How did Mr. Hudson respond?" Lea asked.

"He told me I was the one who needed to get some sense in my head. He said it was the wrong way to go about changing my dad's mind."

"What were his exact words, do you remember?"

"He said 'put down that peashooter and go home, kid.' Like he was talking to a five-year-old. It made me feel like a dope."

"Hudson could be your killer, Tom," Lea said, her voice rising. "After telling Dalton to put the gun away, he followed the boy to make sure he wouldn't get in trouble. That's when he heard the argument and saw his chance to get rid of Albert. He reloaded the gun with a live round, shot Benson, wiped the pistol, and threw it in the bushes."

"I'll buy that," Tom agreed.

"Hold up a minute, Detective," Scott interrupted. "I'd like nothing better than to help you find someone besides Dalton or me to pin this on, but it couldn't be Cliff. He would have been at the steer-wrestling event at the time of the murder."

"What makes you so sure he attended the event?"

"Because he's a judge."

"Sorry, Lea, that blows your theory to pieces," Tom said. "I'll confirm with the other judges, but it sounds like Hudson has an airtight alibi."

"Maybe not!" Lea jumped up. "I have to go."

She bowed to the chief and ran from the sweat lodge.

* * *

When Maddy got the call from her sister, she could hear excitement in Lea's voice. "When we were at the rodeo, you mentioned one of your customers was a judge for the cook-off."

"That's right."

"I want you to call her for me."

"You want to be a judge next year?" Maddy asked, surprised.

"No, but I need some information. I'll tell you what I want you to find out."

"What's this all about?" Maddy asked.

"We may be able to get your cowboy off after all."

Chapter Eighteen

The morning of the sting arrived, and Tom was more than ready for it. He downed two cups of coffee to compensate for a sleepless night. His excitement over the possibility of capturing the Kingpin was enhanced by his anxiety over learning the identity of the mole.

According to the plan, each officer had been given a different address where the witness was being held. Pacing back and forth, Tom watched the surveillance cameras, one focused on each of the buildings. Since the department only had three safe houses, he had assigned the apartment where Amber had been living to the fourth officer suspected of being the mole.

He felt as if he'd jump out of his skin. He couldn't set aside a bad feeling about what was happening. His apprehension got worse when Pat brought his attention to movement on one of the screens.

"Lieutenant, you've got to see this," she said, pointing.

Tom's misgivings about using Amber's apartment were realized when they watched Amber enter the back entrance to the building where she lived.

"What the blazes!" he swore, cracking his knee on the table.

He grabbed his jacket and walked briskly from the room, yelling over his shoulder. "Stay with the cameras, Pat. I'm going to get her out of there. I can't use the back door without a key, so I'll have to go in the front."

* * *

Speeding toward the building, he punched a number into his phone.

"Lea, what the devil is Amber doing at her apartment?"

There was silence before Lea responded.

"I have no idea. I was planning to visit her later, but I haven't talked with her today."

"Did you tell her she could return to her apartment?" Tom asked. His voice was harsh.

"Of course not. She mentioned something about retrieving her date-book, but I made it clear how dangerous that would be."

"Then she's either stupid," Tom shot back, "or shrewd enough to think she can use the book to blackmail her former customers."

"I swear, Tom, I didn't know."

"All right, I'll go pick her up. If this blows our trap, she'll have plenty to answer for."

He disconnected the call before waiting for a response.

* * *

Tom walked over to the stake-out car parked on the street in front of the apartment building and leaned in the open window. "Something's come up. I'm taking the witness to headquarters," he informed the officer. "Wait here until we get back."

Tom ran up the stairs two at a time. Hurrying down the hall to Amber's apartment, he found the door open. He entered cautiously, closing the door without making a sound.

He cast his eyes over the well-kept interior. From what she had told Lea, most of her appointments took place in motel rooms. Only her best customers were allowed inside her apartment.

Although the minimal amount of furniture was tasteful, the living room appeared to be little more than an entry to the bedroom, not a place where much living transpired.

He rapped on the door and called out. "Amber, you here? It's Detective Elliot."

The young woman appeared in the doorway of the bedroom. "Hey, copper. What are you doing here?"

Her attitude matched her sassy attire: cutoff shorts and a sexy see-through blouse.

150

"If you're serious about changing your line of work like you told Lea, you might consider changing your apparel as well," he said, giving her a once-over.

"You don't like?" she teased, adopting an exaggerated modeling pose.

"It draws more attention to your physique than your IQ," Tom said. "What are you doing anyway? You know you aren't supposed to be here."

"Chill out. I came to pick up a few things."

"I thought Lea took you the stuff you needed."

"I missed my crocs." She giggled, holding up a pair of stuffed crocodile slippers. "They keep my toes warm at night."

"C'mon," he said, motioning with his hand. His patience was running thin. "Let's go."

She dropped the slippers into a large shoulder bag but not quickly enough for Tom to miss seeing the black book she slipped into the bag first.

"Wait, I hear someone coming." He pulled out his gun as Amber backed into the bedroom.

When the front door opened a crack, Tom jerked the knob, planting his feet and pointing his gun directly into the face of the intruder.

"Hold on, Lieutenant," the officer said. "It's me."

"What the devil! I told you to wait outside. You almost got your head blown off."

Tom re-holstered his gun, and called the girl. "No more stalling. Let's get out of here."

Amber had almost passed the officer when he grabbed her arm.

"Sorry, Tom. I can't let you take her."

* * *

In one swift movement, the policeman twisted Amber's arm in back of her, turning her into a shield between him and his commanding officer. He pulled a gun and pointed it at her head.

"Hey, you're hurting me," Amber moaned.

"Are you crazy! What do you think you're doing?" Tom asked. His realization of what was unfolding sent a shiver up his spine.

"I thought someone would be here to take care of her by now. Too bad you showed up to take her away, Lieutenant. You're forcing me to take matters into my own hands."

Tom reached for his holster by reflex. The officer waved his gun in the girl's face. "Don't make me do something I don't want to do."

Tom took a step back, spreading his arms at shoulder level. "Take it easy. No one needs to get hurt."

"That's better," the officer said, pulling the gun away from the girl's face.

"Mind if I sit a moment?" Tom asked. "This is a lot to take in."

He sat down, stretched his arms across the back of the couch, and raised an ankle to his knee. He appeared to be a man having a casual conversation with a friend. "I'm sorry it's you, buddy. We've been together a long time."

"I'm sorry, too." The other man lowered his weapon. A slight smile played across his face. "You know how things go. One day everything is great; the next, it's all in the garbage. Pressure builds to a boiling point until you've got to find a way out."

"You never talked to me about any problems you were having. We could have worked something out."

"Not really," the officer said. "I wasn't where I wanted, or needed, to be. I began to realize I wasn't going to get there being a cop."

"Being a cop isn't about reaching a position. It's about serving."

"Yeah, that's how it started, but I've decided it's time to serve a new master, one willing to put my needs first."

"The person you're serving now is the worst kind of scum," Tom said. "I never would have expected you to cross to the other side, especially to join the ranks of our nemesis."

"You're partly to blame," the officer said. "If you would have backed off, I might not have ended up in this position."

"What do you mean?" Tom asked.

"It was your pursuit that made the Kingpin feel he needed a mole at headquarters to stay on top of your investigation. He would have tapped other members of the team eventually. I was lucky enough to be the first one. I took him up on his extremely lucrative offer."

"Blaming me for your own weakness might make you feel better, but I don't know how you sleep at night knowing the officers you ride patrol with every day are willing to put their lives on the line for you."

"I'll admit I've had some sleepless nights, but they'll disappear when I'm a million miles away from this place and all of you."

"I hope you aren't planning on being a cop wherever you're going."

"I'm not stupid. I knew when I got into this that my police career was over. It doesn't mean I won't have other opportunities to make big money."

"I always took you for a smart guy. I can see how wrong I was if you're buying whatever bull the Kingpin's feeding you about any kind of a future. How do you know the gunman hasn't been instructed to take you out when he takes out the witness?

"Now that you've exposed yourself, you've become a liability. You turned on us, he'll expect you to turn on him. Believe me, the only future you have with the Kingpin is six feet under."

"You got it wrong, Lieutenant. I am a smart guy, that's why we're waiting. When his gunman gets here, he'll take out the girl as planned. When he finds you, he'll take you out as well. That's when I'll take care of him."

"You actually believe the Kingpin will let you get away with killing one of his henchmen?"

"I'll be a hero in the Department: the officer who risked his own life to save his Lieutenant. I'll be more valuable than ever to the Kingpin as a mole.

"Who knows, I might be moved up to take your place. I'll finally get the promotion I was never going to get while you were in charge."

"What makes you think I never would have promoted you?" Tom asked.

"From the day the rookie arrived, she's received special treatment. You've given her under-cover assignments and consulted with her on operations."

"If you think Pat and I are privately consulting, how can you be sure this whole assignment isn't a setup to uncover the mole; a sting Pat's in on? In fact, how do you know there aren't surveillance cameras recording this whole scene, which means a squad car is on its way."

At the mention of cameras, the officer's eyes jerked toward the ceiling. Tom dove for the man's knees knocking him backward. The gun fell from his hand and skidded under the couch. Both men jumped to their feet.

A hooded figure barged through the door, a rifle extending from his body like a third arm. He fired. Glass shattered. A blood-curdling scream pierced the air.

"Amber, hide," Tom shouted. He shoved her inside the bedroom sending her sprawling to the floor and slammed the door. He pushed the officer toward the wall and dove behind the couch.

The gunman fired another round. The sound reverberated through the room like a cannon.

The officer tried to stand, staggered, and fell.

Tom grabbed the gun from the floor behind the couch, stood up, and aimed blindly. Both guns blazed as Tom and the gunman fired. The smell of sulfur filled the air.

One man fell to the ground.

The sound of sirens pierced the silence; patrol cars responding to a scene which officers at the precinct had watched in horror as it unfolded on the surveillance camera.

Chapter Nineteen

Lea parked on the frontage road in front of the Hudson ranch. As soon as she saw Cliff Hudson come out of the house and get into his truck, she jumped out of the car and handed the keys to her sister.

"You know what to do. I'm going to the house to talk to Mildred. Follow Cliff and convince him to come back to the house with you, but give me enough time to get Mildred talking."

"I still think this is crazy. Why can't we call Tom and let him do it?"

"Because we have no evidence," Lea said, "which means Tom has nothing to confront them with. This is our only chance."

"Fine," Maddy said, throwing up her hands, "but what if I can't convince Cliff to come back in time to—"

"Just do it. I don't think you want to explain to Paul what's happened to me if you don't."

* * *

Moving as quietly as possible, Lea entered the Hudson house without knocking. She moved toward the sound of clattering dishes in the kitchen.

"Good morning," Lea said, standing in the doorway.

Mildred Hudson spun around, dropping a cup on the floor. The sound of shattering porcelain was heard through the room.

"You startled me," Mildred said. Her tone was decidedly less friendly than on the previous day. "What are you doing here?"

"I was talking with Detective Elliot about your husband yesterday."

"If you two are trying to connect Clifford with Albert's murder, you're wasting your time," she snapped.

"Don't worry; Tom is convinced Mr. Hudson has an airtight alibi. All he needs to do is confirm it with the other judges."

"Then I'll repeat my question," Mildred said. Red color flamed her cheeks. "Why are you here?"

"Because you're the Hudson who doesn't have an air-tight alibi. I confirmed that myself yesterday," Lea said, "but with the judges of the cook-off, not with the judges of the rodeo. Congratulations, Mildred. You won for your ribs just as you'd hoped."

Mildred dropped the tea towel on the counter and braced herself against the edge of the sink with both hands. She looked more like a woman receiving bitter news than a woman being congratulated.

"Too bad you weren't present to receive the ribbon. Your cousin accepted on your behalf."

"I was busy," Mildred said. She looked down, pushing pieces of the broken cup under the table with her foot.

"What could have kept you away from collecting the prize you'd coveted except—"

"Preventing someone from taking away a bigger prize," Mildred said. Her body slumped into a chair at the kitchen table. She clasped her hands, rubbing one hand over the other. "Albert would have ruined everything. I could have lost my husband, my home, and any hopes for a new future."

Lea sat down across from Mildred. She couldn't help but feel the woman's total misery.

"Albert and I had an affair the year before his wife died," Mildred said. "It started when I received an invitation from the Bensons to attend Victoria's showing at a gallery in town. I couldn't coax my husband away from his moronic game shows, so I attended the exhibit alone. Victoria had to stay until the last person left, but she insisted that Albert take the ride home I offered him.

"We stopped to enjoy the sunset, and ended up talking until long after the stars came out." Her gaze wandered to the living room. She stared at the landscape painting hanging above the fireplace.

"Mildred," Lea said gently, drawing the woman's attention back into focus.

"Albert was proud of his wife's talent, but he realized that he and I had more in common. We talked about which crops to plant in the spring rotation, marveled together over newborn sheep, and discussed the latest farm machinery. His wife's passion was for painting landscapes. He and I shared a passion for growing the things she painted.

"Victoria wanted more children, but they had trouble conceiving their first-born. The doctors gave her little hope for another pregnancy. As their hopes for a second child dimmed, she grew more and more into the solitude of her painting. Albert brought his loneliness to me."

"But she was your friend as much as Albert. How could you betray that friendship?"

"She was the kind of woman I wished to be, but wasn't. When I was with Albert, that no longer mattered. She had her art, I had her husband."

Lea was silenced for a moment by the coldness of the woman. "Go on," she said.

"Contrary to the doctor's prognosis, Victoria conceived." Mildred's lips drew into a thin line, and her eyes narrowed. "It was at odds with what Albert led me to believe about their physical relations."

"What did he do?"

"He began feeling guilty, saying it wasn't right to be sneaking around with another woman when his wife was pregnant," Mildred said, unleashing a stream of smoldering acid. "Another woman, that's what he called me, another woman."

"Did your affair survive her dying in childbirth?"

"What do you think? Albert went into a period of grieving he never recovered from. He blamed himself, said her dying was his punishment for being unfaithful. He believed his sin was visited on his children by their growing up without a mother."

"Was Albert worried that his wife knew about your relationship before her death?"

"We were certain she never suspected. In the end, it didn't matter; his guilt destroyed him anyway. He was never the same, devoured by the kind of endless grieving which prevents a person from moving on with their life."

"The affair happened years ago. Why kill him now?" Lea asked.

"The offer to buy his land stirred it all up again. Dalton wanted to move to town and tried to convince his father it would be better for Lucy as well." Mildred stood and paced around the room telling her story. "Albert wanted his children to understand why holding on to the land was so important. The land the family had lived on together was the only thing they had left of Victoria. He got it in his head that his children should know the truth. He wanted to tell them about our affair and how he felt their mother's death was punishment for his adultery."

"Would it have mattered to you? It had been years since the affair as far as explaining it to your husband."

"Years, centuries, it wouldn't have mattered. Clifford has the bull-headed pride of ranchers. What's theirs is theirs. Letting someone take your property is forbidden. He would have made me pay for it the rest of my life."

"But your husband wants to sell the ranch. With your half of the proceeds from the sale, you could leave Clifford and start a new life."

"That's the problem. Clifford inherited all this," Mildred said, spreading her arms. "I have no rights to it."

"Of course; property acquired by inheritance during marriage is legally considered as separate property," Lea said, grasping the woman's dilemma. "But why didn't you have the title changed to community property years ago?"

"We never had a reason. I only considered it when I had my fling with Albert. It was the first time I'd asked myself how I'd get along if I left Clifford or if anything happened to him."

"Did you ask your husband about changing the title?"

"I mentioned it one time. He laughed, saying he'd live to be a hundred, so I had nothing to worry about. I could hardly suggest the other reason. But once Clifford started talking about selling, I realized that if we sold this property and bought another place, the new house would be community property. Half of whatever we bought would be mine, enough to divorce him and start a new life without him."

"What made Clifford decide to sell?"

"The fool ran up a ton of debt trying to set up a hydroponic farming system. The 'wave of the future' he called it. The problem is that it required a large amount of equipment to be purchased. The bank's been calling in loans he can't repay. He has no choice but to sell. Albert stood in the way of that."

"I understand why you felt you needed to get rid of Albert, but why kill him at the rodeo?" Lea asked.

"I figured the perfect opportunity would present itself between the number of ranchers who hated his guts being present at the rodeo as potential suspects and the number of handguns being flashed around for the shooting competitions."

"So you took a pistol with you anticipating an opportunity?"

"I could hardly believe my eyes when I saw what happened between Dalton and his father and realized that I could put my bullets in Dalton's gun to shoot Albert."

"Clever. By not using your own gun, the police wouldn't trace the bullet back to you."

"It turned out better than I'd hoped for." Mildred gloated.

"So you wanted Dalton to be accused of the murder?" Lea asked, slapping her hand on the table. "Your willingness to frame that young man is unbelievable."

"I saw my opportunity, and I took it," Mildred said, offering no sign of remorse. She stopped in front of a closet, reached in, and pulled out a rifle.

Her hands, as she pointed the gun at Lea, were as steady as a rock. Her voice was as cold as a block of ice.

"You didn't tell me the first time we met that you and your sister were the ones my husband caught snooping in the barn. Shame you didn't follow his advice and stay away.

"Actually, I should thank you for discovering the poison and throwing suspicion on my husband as the person responsible for poisoning Albert's crops. It means they're as likely to accuse him of Albert's murder as they are to accuse the boy. Either way, I'll be in the clear."

"You can't believe you'll get away with this. What do you intend to do?"

"We women protect our land same as the men. It's like Clifford told you, we shoot trespassers. The police know about your being found on our property once before; they won't be surprised when it happens again. Only this time, your sister's not around to save you with her fancy martial arts. Let's go out to the barn. I don't want blood spilled on my shiny wood floors."

* * *

Mildred shoved the barrel of the shotgun in Lea's back and pushed her. The screen door flew open hitting the tall figure standing behind it.

The man's face was ashen, his posture rigid like a stone monument. His voice boomed like a crack of thunder.

"You won't be taking her anywhere, woman."

"Clifford, where—"

"This young woman brought me," he said, pointing toward Maddy. "She told me there was something going on at the house I needed to see and hear. She was right," he yelled, raising his arm above his wife's head as if to strike her.

"That's enough, Cliff. We'll take it from here," Maddy said as she walked toward the porch, a shotgun resting on her forearm.

"Where did you get the gun, Maddy?" Lea gasped.

"Pulled it out of his truck. I figured it might come in handy," Maddy said. She pointed it in Mildred's direction. "I know how to use it. I'm an expert marksman in case you think I'm just eye candy."

Mildred's shoulders drooped. She lowered the rifle and turned toward her husband. "I can—"

"Shut your mouth, I don't want to hear another word." He clenched his fists and his jaw turned to granite.

"Do what you want with her," he snapped at Lea and stomped into the house. The screen door slammed behind him.

Mildred slouched into a rocker, dropping her head in her hands.

Lea picked up the barrel of Mildred's rifle with her thumb and forefinger and passed it to her sister. "Call Tom. Tell him to come get Mildred."

"Gladly," Maddy said, punching in a number. "Then I'll call Scott and Katie to let them know this nightmare is over."

Maddy swore under her breath when her call went to voice-mail. "You're never there when I need you, Tom, call me right away." She ended the call, and punched in another number.

Relieved to hear a live voice, the words tumbled out. "Pat, it's Maddy. Lea's cracked the Benson murder. Mildred Hudson has confessed. We're with her at the Hudson ranch. Tell Tom to come pick her up."

"I'll send a car right away, but Tom can't come."

"Can't, or won't? Case of sour grapes over someone else solving the case?"

"Tom set up a bust of the prostitution ring. It went sideways. Two officers were involved in a shooting. They've been taken to the hospital. I'm on my way to the emergency room."

"Tom?" Maddy choked.

"I don't know. I'll call you when I find out. A car will pick up your prisoner momentarily. Kudos," she added hastily, "on catching the murderer."

Maddy clicked off and thrust the rifle into Lea's hands. "Tom's been shot. I'm going to the hospital."

"But—" Lea objected, grasping the weapon gingerly.

"Just channel Dad, you'll be fine. Ride back to town in the squad car," she yelled over her shoulder, racing to Lea's car.

Chapter Twenty

Maddy drove to the hospital unmindful of the speed limit. Tears streamed down her face as she repeated the mantra 'let him be safe' over and over.

She ran to the reception area at the emergency entrance.

"The officer who was brought in," she asked, breathlessly, "where is he?"

"He's in surgery."

Maddy's knees buckled, and she felt light-headed. She braced her hands against the counter.

"What are you doing here?"

She twirled at the sound of the familiar voice.

"You're all right!" she said, grabbing Tom's arms.

He winced and reached for his shoulder. "Ouch, take it easy, woman."

"Omigawd, you're hurt."

"A flesh wound," he said, rubbing a patch on his arm. "It's nothing."

A doctor approached, pulling a surgical mask from his face. "The other officer should recover, but it will be touch-and-go for a few hours."

"And the other man?"

"DOA."

Pat came down the hall. "We're all set, Lieutenant. A guard has been posted at the patient's room. I'll hang around a while to see if he regains consciousness."

"Call me as soon as we can talk to him. I'll head back to headquarters to write up a report and make sure Amber is secure."

"Can I give you a ride?" Maddy asked. Her voice was still shaky.

"Thanks, but someone from the precinct is coming to pick me up."

"You can't go back to work," Maddy argued.

"Don't worry. I'll take the rest of the day off as soon as I've cleared up the loose ends."

"Promise?"

"Promise," Tom said. "Here's my ride now."

"Hey, boss." A broad grin spread across the officer's face. "Glad to see you're still alive and kicking."

"Your concern is touching," Tom said, throwing his good arm around the young man's shoulder. "Let's get out of here. I hate hospitals."

Tom stopped to brush a kiss across Maddy's cheek. "I'll call you tonight. You can come over and nurse me."

The two men walked toward the door.

"Should I consider this a demotion? I used to ride shotgun as your patrol partner. Now, I'm your chauffeur."

"Don't worry, JJ. You're good."

* * *

Tom was ready to keep his promise to Maddy when his phone rang. "Yeah, Pat. What's up?"

"The patient's come to. He's groggy with pain pills but coherent enough to talk."

"I'm on my way."

* * *

Pat was waiting in the reception area when Tom arrived at the hospital. "Room 204."

"Give me a moment," Tom said, taking a deep breath. "I need to calm down. Being confrontational will only make him defensive."

"I know how you feel," Pat said. "When I think he was willing to let you get snuffed, I could shoot him myself."

"Let's find out what he has to say for himself."

The patient was propped up with pillows. Fluids dripped into his arm from a bag hanging on a stand. Spasms of pain rippled across his face when he tried to sit up straighter.

"How you doing?" Tom asked. The callous tone of the question suggested it was rhetorical.

"Do you really care?" Rick's voice was raspy. He cleared his throat. "I'll live. The doctor tells me the bullet passed through without hitting any organs."

"No thanks to your benefactor," Tom said. "I hope it's clear to you by now that the gunman's orders were to take out both you and the girl."

Rick turned toward the wall, grimacing with the effort.

"Geez, man, smarten up," Pat said, throwing her hands in the air. "If Tom hadn't been there to save your sorry ass, you'd be dead."

"I didn't see it going down that way."

"How could you not!" she said. "Did you honestly think being in cahoots with that ruthless bastard wouldn't end up with someone getting hurt?"

"You think I should be grateful?" Rick sneered at Pat and glared at his boss. "You know what happens to cops in jail."

"It doesn't have to be that way," Tom said.

"What do you mean?" Rick asked.

"Help us bring down the Kingpin, and we'll work with the D.A. to reduce your sentence and get you transferred to facilities where you haven't been responsible for putting some of the inmates behind bars."

"What do you think will happen to me if I turn on the Kingpin?" he asked. His eyes were empty, like someone who's run out of hope.

"Your only chance is to get as far away from here as possible," Tom said, "and the only way you can make that happen is to cooperate."

The nurse entered the room. "You'll have to leave, Detective. I need to change his bandages."

"Let me know, Rick. Your time's running out."

* * *

By the time Tom knocked on Maddy's door, it was late. He peeked through the window and saw her dressed in robe and pajamas, lying on the floor in front of the fireplace, sipping a glass of wine. A glowing fire was a frequent sight at Maddy's cottage, less than a block from the ocean where night breezes over the water created chilliness.

"Door's open," she hollered, setting aside her book.

Maddy's house always felt like a safe refuge to Tom, but particularly tonight, after the day he'd put in.

He pulled off his shoes at the door and padded across the wood floor on stocking feet. Dropping down beside her on a padded quilt, he propped himself up on sheepskin cushions. She poured a glass of wine from a bottle on the tray beside her.

He began to unwind with the crackling sound of burning logs, the sight of smoke trailing up the chimney, and the sweet smell of lavender-scented candles.

"How's the arm?" she asked.

"Now that I have time to notice," he admitted, "it's smarting a little." He stretched his legs out, closed his eyes, and took a deep breath.

Maddy watched as burrows across his forehead melted away like butter. His shoulder and neck muscles loosened, and his breathing became shallower.

"I had quite a scare when Pat told me officers were down," she told him.

"Sorry you heard about it that way, not knowing if it was me or not."

"I may have run a red light or two driving to the hospital," she admitted, watching the corners of his mouth turn up. "When I think of how many promises I made to the higher powers—"

"The higher powers must have enjoyed that, especially coming from someone who answers to no one."

"You're making fun of me." She reached to poke him but withdrew when he flinched. "Sorry, but seriously, you've always seemed invincible to me. Like my father, until the day he had his stroke and I realized he wasn't invincible at all. Today, I found out you aren't invincible either."

"I tell myself I'm indestructible," Tom said. He gazed into her eyes with heart-pounding intensity. "But I've learned I'm not invulnerable to pain."

"I don't know how to process what happened. I never worried about you before. I don't know what's worse; the thought of worrying about you all the time or the thought of losing you."

"Now you know how I feel when you tell me not to worry about you."

Maddy smiled. "Yeah, I get it."

"What are you trying to tell me, Maddy?" Tom asked, sitting up.

"I'm not sure except our relationship has changed colors, for me, anyway."

"What's the color of our relationship now?"

"Richer…deeper…darker."

"In case you hadn't noticed, our relationship's already been there for me."

"I felt you'd begun to see us differently, but it made me uncomfortable. I didn't know what to do with that."

"Do you know now?"

"Well, I—"

A chirping sound came from the phone clipped to Tom's belt. "It's a call from the hospital."

A moment later, Tom replaced his phone and leaned over to kiss her. "Rick wants to talk, I've got to go."

* * *

Maddy's phone rang a short time later.

"Are we okay?" Tom asked.

"I'm more upset with your running around with a bad shoulder than your leaving," Maddy told him.

"You think Lea's still got tickets to the Pier shindig?"

"She held on to a couple in case I changed my mind. How many do you need?" she asked, holding her breath.

"Two, assuming you're willing to have a man with a bum wing as an escort."

"An evening by the ocean, eating gourmet food, and drinking wine. Yeah, I think I can handle that. Besides, when have I ever been unwilling where you're concerned?"

"Good to hear. Wear something sparkly. I'll pick you up at eight." He rang off.

Chapter Twenty-One

Tom paid the attendant at the parking lot and grumbled under his breath. "Twice the usual price. Good thing we got comp tickets from Lea or I'd be set back a month's wages for this shindig."

Maddy laughed. "Think of all the money you're saving by tasting samples of the different cuisines instead of taking me to dinner at the chefs' restaurants."

"It's not only the menu prices but the dress codes which keep me from their places," Tom said, running a finger under his starched shirt collar.

"I hope you don't regret coming," Maddy said. She pursed her lips in a succulent pout as he helped her out of the car.

He looked at the curvaceous figure draped in a skin-tight cocktail dress, the chestnut hair flowing over strapless shoulders, and the flawless, glowing complexion.

"How could I have misgivings about spending the night with the most beautiful woman in the county?"

"You're a charmer when you want to be, Tom Elliot," Maddy said, soaking in the compliment.

Walking onto the promenade, they saw rows of white canopies equipped with serving tables, chafing dishes, and warming trays. Chefs dished up servings of coconut shrimp, seared scallops, ravioli, pork medallions, and beef tenderloin. Waiters dressed in black pants and white shirts walked through the crowd carrying trays loaded with small plates of bruschetta with salsa and melted brie, sausage roll-ups, mini tacos, and spring rolls.

Moonlight reflected off glasses partially filled with varieties of red and white wine.

Waves of music performed by a string quartet blanketed the crowd.

Tom saw the chief of police standing at the center of a large group of people and stopped to shake hands. "Good evening, Superintendent."

"Good to see you, Lieutenant, although I'll admit, I'm a bit surprised. It's not often we see you in a coat and tie."

"I need a good reason to put on a monkey suit," Tom answered.

"I see your reason tonight," the police chief said.

Tom blushed and shuffled his feet. "You remember Maddy."

The superintendent nodded and turned his eyes back to his lieutenant. "I heard about the incident yesterday. How are you, shouldn't you be taking some time off?"

"I appreciate your concern, but I'm fine."

"Well, enjoy the event. It's a beautiful evening, and you have a beautiful date. Take it easy and relax."

"I'll do my best, sir. Thank you."

* * *

Tom and Maddy were filling their plates with delicacies when a man stepped up behind them.

"Would you mind leaving some for the rest of us?"

Tom spun around. Paul grinned and reached for a plate. "How you doing, pal? I heard you got your wing clipped yesterday."

"Good thing our softball team has an ace hitter for a replacement. I may have to sit out a game or two."

"I hope your sacrifice paid off."

"We'll know sooner than later," Tom said. He turned toward Lea and Maddy and raised his glass. "Here's to the two best amateur sleuths in the county."

"That's a back-handed compliment if I ever heard one," Lea said.

"You never did tell me how you were able to find Dalton."

"It was easy. I thought of the best one to find me if I ran away or got lost."

"Me?" Paul guessed.

"Better than you," Lea said. "Gracie or Spirit. So I used Dalton's dog, Rascal."

"I hate to tell you this, but you've blown your chance of ever running away," Maddy said. "You've told us how to find you."

"I'm only glad we found Dalton before he did something drastic," Lea said.

"He may not have been the only one you saved by finding Albert's murderer," Paul told her.

"What do you mean?"

"Once Mildred had the financial means to live on her own, she would have been free to leave her husband. If she had trouble getting a divorce, she might have turned into a black widow."

"You're right," Lea said. She felt goose bumps on her arms. "By getting rid of Cliff, she'd get the rest of his money."

"I'm grateful for your help, Lea," Tom said.

"I got my reward. I won the contract to do the grand opening for Jim Mitchell's condominium project, and I stand a good chance of working on promotions for his ranchette project."

"Is it going through?" Tom asked.

"The Millers have agreed to sell their parcel in order to make sure Dalton gets an offer."

"That was generous of them," Tom said. He finished the finger food on his plate. "I'm ready for the main course."

"You're out of luck, pal," Paul said. "That was the main course."

Maddy caught the arm of a waiter carrying a tray filled with cupcakes, mini cheesecakes, and tarts. "Hold on there, fella. You've got what I'm looking for."

"There's Pat," Lea said, waving toward the entrance where Pat and JJ were discretely presenting credentials at the entrance booth.

Tom lowered Lea's hand. "They're not here for the festivities."

His face took on a somber expression as he looked toward his officers with no more than a subtle nod. He was pleased to see they were dressed for the occasion. He watched them weave their way through the crowd without attracting undue attention.

Failing to notice his change in mood, Maddy offered Tom a cream puff.

He brushed it away with his hand. "There's one more entree I need to sample before I'll be ready for dessert."

* * *

Tom walked toward a table where a man dressed in white and wearing a chef's hat filled plates for people standing in line. The insignia on his shirt matched the banner above the canopy: 'Bluff Resort'.

A tall, angular man with a beaked nose stood beside the chef. He wore a white tuxedo with a red pocket handkerchief. Close by was a hefty man wearing a suit cut full enough in the chest to conceal a firearm.

Tom joined the back of the line. He watched the man in the white tux intently, savoring the moment. As he neared the table, the detective stepped out of line to stand in front of him.

"You must be Teddy Vincent, owner of the Bluff Resort," Tom said cordially. "I've heard great things about your world-class restaurant. Tell me, does the name of your resort refer to its location on the cliff above the ocean or the legitimacy of your business?"

"Most of my clientele call me Theodore," the man responded in a chilly voice.

"I'm not one of your customers, and that's not the way your name shows up under the mug shot back in Chicago."

The man's body went rigid. The blood drained from his face.

"My counterparts in the windy city have been looking for you for some time. Was it the climate which brought you out here or the fact that they were breathing down your neck? They're going to be real happy to get their hands on you."

"This is an outrage. You're mistaking me for someone else," Teddy sputtered. He looked over his shoulder.

Tom saw movement out of the corner of his eye seconds before the bodyguard grabbed his wounded arm.

"Is this gentleman bothering you, sir?" the muscle-man asked, twisting the detective's arm behind his back. Tom grimaced in pain.

"Escort him off the premises," Teddy ordered. "He's convinced I'm someone other than who I am."

As the bodyguard steered Tom away from the canopy, JJ pushed a gun into the thug's side. "You aren't taking the Lieutenant anywhere."

Tom jerked away from the man's grasp and turned back to Teddy.

"Teddy Vincent, I'm arresting you on charges of illegal gambling, drug trafficking, and prostitution."

A crowd of people was gathering. Teddy spotted the police chief.

"Is this one of your men, Superintendent? I demand to be released immediately." Saliva spewed out of his mouth.

Everyone froze in place. The Superintendent looked from one man to the other.

"Detective Elliot isn't prone to making mistakes. I think I'll leave it to him to sort out." The police chief turned and walked away.

Pat and JJ marched off with the Kingpin and his bodyguard in tow.

Tom approached Maddy. "I've got to—"

"I know. You've got to go. Don't worry. I'll get a ride home with Lea."

Tom walked toward the parking lot where a police van was parked.

"Abandoned again," Maddy sighed, turning to her sister. "Give me a moment, and then let's go find the waiter with the goodies tray. I feel like drowning my sorrow in sweets."

* * *

Maddy walked to the end of the pier and sat on a bench, watching the fiery red sun dip slowly into the ocean. She felt the moistness of the sea air as the breeze blew her long hair away from her face and breathed deeply, inhaling the clean, salty tang. She closed her eyes, letting the glowing sun fade to an orange dot on the back of her eyelids.

"It's a beautiful evening, isn't it? Mind if I join you?"

She opened her eyes and turned toward the voice behind her. It was Scott's mother, dressed in an elegant green dress accented by a necklace of sparkling gemstones.

"Nice to see you, Claire. Please, come enjoy the sunset."

They sat quietly for a moment enjoying the fusion of sounds created by the ocean waves and the string quartet.

"Did Scott come?" Maddy asked. "I haven't seen him."

"No, he doesn't like these events much."

"I don't know many men who do."

"Have you sampled the dishes?" Claire asked.

"Yes, I've stuffed myself already, but I'll probably go back for pastries. I admit to having a sweet tooth."

"I'm guilty of one as well, but I lean more toward chocolates."

Both women smiled, comfortable in each other's presence.

"Speaking of guilt, I'd like to thank you and your sister for clearing Scott with the police. Of course, he was innocent, but the cloud of suspicion hanging over him was a strain on all of us."

"I'm sorry you had to go through that experience, but the police were only doing their job," Maddy said. She was surprised at how readily she came to Tom's defense.

"We understood that," Claire said, "but it didn't make it any easier. I'm glad the whole nasty business is behind us."

"How's Lucy? Is she still staying with you?"

"Yes, she is. Katie insisted, and we're glad to have her. She and Katie have been as close as sisters since Scott and Katie moved back home. The girls share the bond of growing up without a mother."

"And Dalton?"

"I'm happy to say he's staying with us, too. He goes to the Benson farm every day to take care of things but after he finishes his work, he has dinner with us and stays the night."

"Are they planning to move into town?"

"Dalton's already found an apartment. They'll be moving as soon as escrow closes on the sale of the farm. Katie will miss having Lucy so close, but they see each other at school and Lucy will spend part of the summer with us. It's all working out nicely."

"Dalton's a good boy," Maddy said. "I'm sorry he lost his father, but I think he's got a happier future ahead of him."

"I agree. Scott will make sure the boy stays on track and gets his degree, but Dalton's always been level-headed and self-motivated. I think he'll do fine."

Claire ran her fingers back and forth over her necklace. "Things may have worked out for the best. Dalton would have left his father eventually, but he would have done so burdened with either a continuing responsibility to help with the farm or the pain of a broken relationship if he refused."

"I guess it's true that sometimes a greater good results from a terrible loss."

"If not a greater good, at least, a sense of peace."

Maddy knew Claire was no longer referring to Dalton but to her son.

Claire looked directly at Maddy and smiled. "You've been a good friend to Scott."

Maddy didn't miss the reference to her as a friend. She sensed the other woman was choosing her words carefully.

"It's sad what happened to Albert after he lost Victoria. I lost my husband suddenly as well, but I didn't suffer the endless grieving Albert put himself through. Rather than being bitter over the loss, I was grateful for the years we'd had together."

"I'm sure that's the way a spouse who passes would want to be remembered."

For a moment, Claire let her eyes drift toward the setting sun. "Memories of my husband are never associated with pain. He was the love of my life, and I was the love of his. He made me feel that his life revolved around me. All he needed for a perfect day was for me to be in it."

She returned her gaze to Maddy. "I'm happy my son was fortunate enough to share years of his life with a woman he loved so deeply."

"Are you saying a person experiences only one perfect love in their lifetime?"

"Not at all," Claire said. "I'm not saying Scott won't find another big love, but it could never be the same kind of love. Of course, Katie's the center of his universe now."

She searched the other woman's face. "What about you, Maddy? Have you experienced being the love of someone's life?"

"Not with my ex-husband. Eric didn't need me for the woman I was, he only needed a woman. Any woman who complemented him would have filled the bill."

"There is no feeling more gratifying than knowing you're the center of someone's universe. I hope you find that someday."

Maddy stared out over the ocean at the reflection of a rising moon shimmering on the water. She experienced a moment of total peace.

"Thank you, Claire. I believe I have already."

* * *

The sisters were sipping champagne and munching strawberries dipped in chocolate when an arm circled Maddy's waist. She spun around.

Tom loosened his tie and stuffed it in his pocket. "Let's blow this bash."

Maddy took off her heels and handed them to her sister. "Take care of these for me. I won't be needing them anymore tonight."

Tom and Maddy walked down the stairs to the beach.

<<<<>>>>

A Sister Sleuths Mystery: Book One

Sisters Lea, a freelance business writer, and Maddy, an interior designer, are sticking their noses into the murder Lea's adventurous canines discovered under the Pier in their peaceful beach community.

There's no shortage of suspects since the victim was despised by several people in town including a humiliated fiancé jilted at the altar, angry co-workers frustrated by his undeserved success, a married lover, an employee wrongfully terminated, and dangerous criminal associates.

You're guaranteed to love the sisters' spunk, intelligence, and tenacity as well as the twists and turns of this intriguing plot. These irrepressible siblings are up to the challenge and only stop when the mystery is solved.

A Sister Sleuths Mystery: Book Two

The second book in the "Sister Sleuths Mystery" series presents Lea, Maddy, and Detective Tom with at least one body, several suspects, and plenty of motives.

The local community theatre in their beachside town provides the backdrop and a provocative cast of suspects including an arrogant actor, a business partner anxious to sell, a stage manager with a gambling addiction, and a cunning wife who would like to get rid of both the theatre and her husband.

The clues are there for the observant but the final revelations are sure to surprise. The tight, pacy plot leads the reader through many twists and turns, and the result is a whodunit with a completely unpredictable ending.

From the Author

To receive updates on my latest author news, book releases, and special price offers, please subscribe to my Book Alerts at http://www.raynamorgan.info/

Dear Reader,

Thank you for joining Lea, Maddy, and the dogs in their sleuthing adventures.

If you enjoyed your time spent with them, would you please consider posting a review on Amazon? Reviews are very helpful to other readers and are greatly appreciated.

If you have questions or comments, I can be reached at raynamorgan2@gmail.com and would love to hear from you.

Also, if you encounter typos or errors in this book, please send them to me at this email address. Even with all the editing, mistakes can slip through. With your help, I can correct them for future readers.

Thank you!

Rayna

Made in the USA
Coppell, TX
11 June 2021

57259567R00105